# The Beach Club Volume I
# MAGIC BEACH
## T. Johnson

outskirts press
DENVER, COLORADO

The Beach Club Volume I
Magic Beach
All Rights Reserved.
Copyright © 2013 T. Johnson
v4.0

Cover Photo © 2013 Tim Johnson. All rights reserved - used with permission.
Illustrations by John Brennan

Outskirts Press, Inc.
http://www.outskirtspress.com

ISBN: 978-1-4327-9316-6

Outskirts Press and the "OP" logo are trademarks belonging to Outskirts Press, Inc.

PRINTED IN THE UNITED STATES OF AMERICA

# Chapter 1
# School's Out

It was the last day of school and Mikey was counting down the seconds.

"Three... Two... One..."

RRRRIIIIIINNNNGG! The school bell sounded and 5th grade was history. All of the kids screamed with joy as Mr. Jackson yelled over the noise, "Have a great summer everyone. I'll see you all in September!"

Mr. Jackson was Mikey's favorite teacher. Somehow he always seemed to make English class interesting. That's something no other teacher had been able to do for Mikey. So he made a point of stopping by Mr. Jackson's desk on his way out.

"Have a nice summer Mr. Jackson."

"You too Mikey. Make it one to remember so you'll have something to write about in English class next year."

"Okay Mr. Jackson. See ya!"

And with that Mikey threw his book bag on his shoulder and dashed out of the room. As he ran down the hall toward the stairs, he ran right past the Principal, without even noticing her.

The principal yelled out "MIGUEL FRANCISCO SANCHEZ!"

Mikey froze in his tracks. The sound of his full name always sent chills up his spine. He turned around to see her standing in the middle of the hall.

"Come here young man!" the principal said in a stern voice.

Mikey slowly walked back to the principal. "Yes ma'am?" he gulped.

The principal looked him square in the eyes and said, "Just because this is the last day of school, it does not mean you can run through the halls like a wild animal. Now I want you to turn around and walk back down the hall like a civilized young man. Do I make myself clear?"

"Yes ma'am," Mikey answered, as he turned and began to walk calmly down the hall.

"And Mikey…" the principal began to add with a smile on her face, "I'll be home a little late today. I have some loose ends to tie up around here before *my* summer vacation begins."

"Okay Ma," Mikey smiled, "I'll see you later."

Principal Sanchez blew Mikey a kiss and whispered, "See you later Pookie."

Mikey's face turned red with embarrassment. "Aw Ma," he said as he turned to see if anyone might have overheard his mother's comment. To his relief there was no one else around. Mikey gave a sigh of relief and headed back down the hall. Being the son of the principal wasn't always easy.

Mikey hurried down the stairs so he could meet his friend Curtis in front of the school. They always sat together on the bus. They lived in the same apartment building on the other side of town. When Mikey came outside Curtis was there waiting.

"What took you so long?" asked Curtis.

"Let's just say, I got snagged by the principal," Mikey replied.

"Ah. Say no more," said Curtis. "All that matters is that we didn't miss the bus. Here it comes now."

The two boys boarded the bus and compared baseball cards all the way home.

When Mikey reached his Newark, New Jersey apartment he let himself in with his key. He couldn't wait to get started with his summer vacation. As soon as he walked in the door, he discarded his bookbag, as well as his sneakers and socks. He ran to the kitchen and made himself a bowl of Fruity Flakes. Fruity Flakes was Mikey's favorite cereal. He could eat them for breakfast, lunch, dinner, or even a quick between-meal snack. Mikey carried his bowl into the living room, hopped on the couch, and turned on the TV. Normally, he wasn't allowed to watch TV until his homework was done. But since this was the last day of school, he figured he was free to watch cartoons to his heart's content. Just as he had gotten comfortable, the telephone rang. It was Curtis. It was customary for Curtis to call after dinner, but since he didn't have any homework either, the call came early today. Mikey answered the phone.

"Hello."

"Hey, it's me," Curtis replied.

"What's up?"

"Nothin'. I was just calling to see what you were doing."

"I'm just watching TV," Mikey said. "The Power-Botts are on."

"I know," said Curtis. "I'm watching them too. It's a rerun. I've seen this one before. Wanna go outside and ride bikes?"

"I can't," Mikey said. "I'm not allowed to go out until my Mom gets home." Besides, Mikey had never seen this episode of the Power-Botts and he really wanted to see how it ended.

"Well she should be home soon, right?" asked Curtis.

"I don't know," Mikey replied. "She said she had some stuff to do at school and she would be home late."

"How late?" asked Curtis.

"She didn't say," Mikey replied. "I'm sure it won't be too late."

"That kinda stinks," Curtis said. But Mikey didn't mind. He had the whole apartment to himself for a while. He sort of liked that. Besides, he had his cartoons to keep him company.

There was a brief moment of silence while the two boys watched TV, then Curtis asked Mikey, "So what are you going to do this summer?"

Mikey wasn't really paying attention because the

cartoon he was watching had gotten to the exciting part and he was on the edge of his seat.

"Mikey? You still there?" Curtis asked.

Mikey snapped back to reality. "Huh? Oh… yeah. What did you say?"

"I asked you what you were going to do this summer," Curtis repeated.

Mikey hadn't really thought about it. "What do you mean?" he asked.

"Well," Curtis started, "my dad said he's going to take my brother and me to an amusement park next week and a water park the week after that. And next month the whole family is going on a vacation to the Grand Canyon. So what are you guys planning to do?"

Mikey felt a little jealous. He didn't have a big family to do things with. He didn't have any brothers or sisters, or a dad for that matter. It was just him and his mother. And as far as he knew, they didn't have any big plans for the summer. But he felt obligated to answer Curtis's question.

"Um… My ma and I haven't made any plans for the summer… yet… We're going to talk about it when she gets home."

"Oh," said Curtis. "Well call me back later and tell me what you guys decide to do. Okay?"

"Okay," Mikey replied. "I'll call you back after dinner. Later."

"Later," replied Curtis and he hung up.

Mikey sat on the couch for a while thinking of things he might like to do during the summer. Then he remembered what Mr. Jackson told him as he walked out of class that day. *'Make it one to remember so you'll have something to write about in English class next year.'* Suddenly Mikey hopped up and ran into his room. He sat down at his desk, pulled out a piece of paper and a pencil and began to make a list of ideas. At the top of the page he wrote in big letters "MY SUMMER WISH LIST".

## Chapter 2
# The Wish List

About an hour went by, and Mikey's mom finally came home. When she opened the door, the first thing she saw was Mikey's sneakers, socks, and book bag scattered all over the floor. The TV was on and there was a half-eaten bowl of Fruity Flakes on the coffee table. Mikey was nowhere to be seen.

"Miguel Francisco Sanchez, come out here right now!"

Mikey cringed. That was the second time today she had used his full name. He figured now was not a good time to show her his summer wish list. He folded up the piece of paper and shoved it into his pocket. Then he hurried into the living room to see what his mother wanted.

"Yes Ma?"

"Mikey, look at this mess you left in here. Now I want you to turn off the TV, pour out the rest of that cereal and put the bowl in the sink. Put your book bag away, pick up those shoes and socks and put them where they belong. Then I want you to clean up your room, because I know it's a wreck. After you are finished all of that, I want you to come back out here because I have a surprise for you."

Mikey quickly started on his tasks. "Yes Ma. I'm sorry Ma. I'll have everything cleaned up in a jiffy Ma." Mikey turned off the TV, poured out the rest of his cereal, scooped up his things and hurried off to his room. He then proceeded to clean his room like it had never been cleaned before. He figured if he did a really good job, his mother might agree to do some of the things that were on his wish list. When he was done he called her into his room for an official inspection. She was very impressed. Mikey was glad. Just then, the doorbell rang.

"Well," she said, "you've got good timing. It looks like your surprise has arrived."

At the door was a pizza deliveryman, and in his hands was a large pepperoni, garlic, and anchovy pizza. Mikey's favorite! He loved pepperoni, garlic, and anchovy pizza almost as much as Fruity Flakes.

"Wahooo!" Mikey yelled. "Let's eat!"

As they ate they talked and laughed. They even had a burping contest. Mikey won easily. He always did.

After dinner Mikey offered to help his mom with the dishes. He figured that would be a good time to spring his wish list on her. She was pleasantly surprised by his offer.

"Okay," she said. "I'll wash and you dry."

"You got it!" Mikey replied. As they were doing the dishes, Mikey looked up at his mother and said, "Hey Ma. I've been thinking."

"Oh? About what Pookie?" she asked.

"Summer vacation," replied Mikey.

"Really?" she said. "That's funny, because I have too."

"You have?" Mikey's eyes gleamed with hope.

Maybe his mother had already come up with some great ideas of her own. Maybe she even came up with some of the same ideas he had.

"Yes I have," she replied. "You see, I'm going to be needed at the school this summer."

"For what?" Mikey asked.

"For summer school," His mother replied.

Mikey suddenly saw his hopes for a great summer vacation going down hill. "Well, how long does summer school last?"

"Throughout the month of July," his mother answered.

"Then we still have the rest of June and all of August to hang out together, right?"

"Sure we do Pookie," she replied. Mikey's hopes were slightly renewed. But he still wasn't sure how the whole summer school thing was going to work out. Maybe, he would be left in control of the apartment while his mom was at school. That would be great. He could watch cartoons all day.

"So I guess for the month of July I'll just be hanging out here until you come home everyday, huh?"

"Well, no. I don't think so honey. That is a little too much time for you to be by yourself."

Mikey was a little disappointed. Thoughts of a babysitter began to pop into his head. He didn't want a babysitter. They were for babies. Mikey was 11 now he could take care of himself. After all, he had his own key to the apartment and everything. But before he could say another word, his mother told him, "I came up with a better idea."

"What?" he asked.

"Do you remember your Auntie Carla and Uncle Tito in North Carolina?"

"Of course," replied Mikey. He always looked forward to seeing them during the holidays.

"Well they just bought a new house. And guess what… It's right on the beach!"

"Cool!" Mikey loved the beach.

"So," his mother continued, "Your Auntie and I were thinking …"

"Yeah…" Mikey interjected. He could see where this was leading and he liked it.

"maybe you…"

"YEAH…" Mikey could barely contain himself. His eyes grew bigger by the second.

"could spend the month of July…"

"YEAH, YEAH…" The poor kid was about to burst with anticipation.

"with your Auntie and Uncle in their new house on the beach in North Carolina!"

"OH YEAH! SWEEEET!" Mikey jumped out of his seat and began to dance around the apartment. "This is going to be awesome! This will be the best summer vacation ever! I have to call Curtis!" He grabbed the telephone and ran off to his room.

Mikey's mother took her cell phone from her pocketbook and called her sister Carla in North Carolina. "Hi Carla," she said as her sister answered the phone.

"Hi Maria. How did things go with Mikey?"

"A lot better than I expected actually. I've never seen him so excited. I probably didn't even need to butter him up with that pepperoni, garlic, and anchovy pizza. He's thrilled. In fact he's in his room right now telling his best friend all about it. Here listen."

Mikey's mother crept down the hall to Mikey's room. The door was cracked and she could hear him talking to Curtis. She held up her cell phone so her sister could listen too.

Mikey was lying on his bed telling Curtis how cool his summer vacation was going to be. He was so excited, he forgot all about the summer wish list that was sticking out of his pocket.

# Chapter 3

# The Arrival

It was the last Sunday in June. Mikey was taking the train to North Carolina today because his mother had to report bright and early for summer school the next day. It seemed like he had been riding on that train forever. The rocking motion of the car and click clack sound of the tracks made him a little sleepy. Besides, Mikey hadn't slept a wink the night before. He was too excited about his trip. But even though he was tired he was still unable to sleep. He was still excited and a little nervous, since this was the first time he had ever traveled alone.

The conductor walked through the door at the end of the train car and announced in a loud voice, "Next stop, Jacksonville Station."

Mikey sat up in his seat. The conductor noticed his excitement and said to him, "Yep. That's you little man. I'll be back to help you with your bag in a minute."

The conductor had helped Mikey get his suitcase on the train earlier that day. That bag was almost as big as he was. His mother had bought him a whole new wardrobe for the summer, and she managed to shove everything into one suitcase.

"Geez Ma," he said to her as he watched her pack his clothes on Saturday, "with all the clothes you're shoving in there, I could wear a different outfit everyday and never have to wash clothes."

The train began to slow down. Mikey looked out

of the window. He could see the station just ahead. He looked to the back of the car to see if the conductor was coming back, but he had gone to the next car and Mikey couldn't see him. So he decided to try and handle the bag himself. The conductor had stuffed it in the overhead compartment over his seat. Mikey stood up in his seat and started to tug at the bag handle. It didn't budge. Mikey wiped the sweat off of his palms, gritted his teeth, and yanked the handle with all of his might. It still didn't budge. Mikey was starting to get angry. But just before he blew a fuse, he heard the conductor's voice.

"Hey little man! I told you I would be back. Couldn't wait huh? Here, let me get that for you." The conductor gave the bag a yank and it came right out.

"Whoa!" said Mikey. He was very impressed. But of course the guy was three times as big as Mikey.

The train came to a stop at the station. "Right this way sir," the conductor said to Mikey. "Is this your first time in North Carolina?"

"No," Mikey replied, "but the last time was about two years ago, when I was just a kid."

"Oh I see," said the conductor.

"Yeah," Mikey went on, "My Auntie and Uncle used to live in Middleton back then. But now they have a house in Cape Vernon, right on the beach."

"Cool," said the conductor.

"Very cool," added Mikey. This visit should be a lot more fun than the last one."

The two stepped off the train. Mikey looked around for his Auntie and Uncle. His mother told him they would meet him at the station.

Just then he heard a familiar voice calling his name. It was his Auntie Carla. She and his Uncle Tito were rushing toward him.

"Do you know these two?" the conductor asked Mikey jokingly.

"Yep!" laughed Mikey. "That's my Auntie Carla and Uncle Tito"

"Oh really?" the conductor said with a smile. "I would have never guessed."

Auntie Carla and Uncle Tito ran up to Mikey and gave him a big hug.

"Welcome to North Carolina!" said Uncle Tito.

"We missed you so much," said Auntie Carla. Look at how big you've gotten."

Uncle Tito took the giant suitcase from the conductor and gave him a tip. Then the three of them went to the parking lot.

As they got in the car Auntie Carla turned to Mikey and said, "I just know you're going to love it at our new house. We have the guest room all set up for you."

"Yeah," Uncle Tito added, "But you're going to have to wait a little longer to see it. Cape Vernon is about 45 minutes from here."

Mikey really was looking forward to seeing his Aunt and uncle's new house, but most of all, he was looking forward to the beach. Thoughts of running barefoot across the sand, diving into the ocean waves, and trips to the boardwalk were racing through Mikey's head. And before he knew it, for the first time in 24 hours, Mikey was sound asleep.

Forty five minutes later, Mikey awoke to the sound of his Uncle Tito's voice, "Mikey. Wake up buddy. We're here." Mikey opened his eyes and looked out of the car window. He found himself in the driveway of a beautiful, 2 story, white house with blue shutters on the windows. There was a porch with a hammock on the side of the house. The porch wrapped all the way around to the back of the house. Mikey was very impressed. He opened the car door and paused for a second as the smell of the ocean air captured his attention.

"Come on," said Auntie Carla "I'll show you the inside."

She and Mikey started walking toward the house as Uncle Tito struggled with the suitcase.

"Geez Mikey!" Uncle Tito said. "With all the clothes you have in here, you could wear a different outfit everyday and never have to wash clothes."

"I know!" laughed Mikey, "That's the same thing I told my mom yesterday."

Auntie Carla led Mikey up the front steps and through two beautiful wood doors into the foyer where Mikey paused again. The inside was just as beautiful as the outside. Mikey stood there for a minute and admired the wood floors, big windows, and stylish furniture. It was the kind of house he had always said he was going to by for himself when he got older.

"Do you like it?" his Auntie asked."

"Yeah," Mikey said in amazement. "This is pretty sweet."

Just then he saw something that made his jaw drop. He began to run straight through to the back of the house. He darted past the living room; past the dining room; past the stair; past the family room; through the kitchen and out of the sliding glass door. He finally stopped at the railing on the edge of the porch in back of the house. There it was at last. The ocean! Mikey had finally made it to the beach! He couldn't contain his excitement another minute. He immediately ran down back steps of the porch onto the beach. He yanked off his sneakers and socks and ran down the beach toward the water.

"Yahoooo!" he yelled as he zigzagged back and forth across the sand. When he reached the ocean, he wadded out to where the water was up to his knees and began to kick, splash and jump over the waves. He stopped for a minute to catch his breath and feel the warm sunlight on his face. He closed his eyes and listened to the waves crash into the shore. He heard a flock of seagulls flying by. They almost seemed to be calling his name. Just then, he realized someone really *was* calling his name. It was his Auntie Carla. She was standing on the porch calling Mikey back to the house. Reluctantly, Mikey walked back to the house.

"Did I do something wrong?" he asked.

"No silly," replied Auntie Carla. "I just thought you might have more fun if you were wearing a bathing suit."

"Oh yeah," said Mikey. He almost forgot he was still wearing a polo shirt and shorts.

"Come on upstairs and change," said Auntie Carla. "I'll get you a towel. Then you can play on the beach while I make dinner."

Mikey went up to his room. It was on the back of the house so he had a great view of the ocean. He changed into one of the swimsuits his mother had packed, and ran back down the steps into the kitchen where Auntie Carla was waiting with a towel. She was on the phone so Mikey just grabbed the towel off the counter and stepped outside the sliding glass door. But before Mikey could get off of the porch, his aunt stopped him.

"Wait a minute Mikey. I have someone who wants to talk to you." She handed him the phone.

"Hello?" he said.

"Hi Pookie," answered the voice on the other end. It was his mother. His Auntie Carla had called her to let her know Mikey had arrived safely.

"Hi Ma!" said Mikey. He was glad to hear her voice.

"How was the trip? You weren't too scared riding by yourself were you?"

"Of course not Ma," Mikey rolled his eyes like he always did whenever he thought his mother was babying him. "Everything was fine."

"Good. So what do you think of Auntie Carla and Uncle Tito's new house?" she asked.

"It's cool. You'd love it Ma. You have to come down and see it sometime," he replied.

"You're right," she said. I do have to come down and see it. Well I'm not going to hold you too long. Your Auntie Carla told me you were on your way out for a swim. Just remember to mind your Aunt and Uncle, and have fun. I'll see you in five weeks. I love you Pookie."

"I love you too Ma."

Mikey gave the phone back to his Auntie, raced down the steps and down the beach, and into the water. He jumped and swam and splashed around until his fingers were pruned while his Uncle Tito watched from the porch. It was the best day of his summer so far, and the fun was just beginning.

## Chapter 4
# What's A Shoobie?

Mikey woke a little later than usual the next day. All of the excitement and fun from the day before left him exhausted by bedtime, and his body needed a little extra sleep to make up for it. When he finally got out of bed, he went downstairs to the family room where his Auntie Carla was reading the morning paper. His Uncle Tito had left for work, so it was just the two of them.

"Well good morning sleepy head," she said. "I thought you'd never wake up. Would you like some breakfast?"

"Sure," said Mikey. "I don't suppose you have Fruity Flakes do you?"

"As a matter of fact I do" Auntie Carla replied to Mikey's surprise. "Your mother told me that was your favorite, so I stocked the cabinets with enough Fruity Flakes to last all month."

"All right!" said Mikey.

"It's a beautiful morning," Auntie Carla said as she walked Mikey to the kitchen. "Would you like to eat out on the porch?"

"Yeah," Mikey replied. "That would be cool."

"Okay," said Auntie Carla. She grabbed two glasses from the cabinet and a carton of orange juice from the refrigerator. She handed them to Mikey and said, "Take these out to the table. I'll get the Fruity Flakes and meet you out there.

Mikey went out on the back porch. To his left was

a round table, with four chairs. Mikey set the glasses on the table, poured the orange juice, and took a seat. Auntie Carla came out with two bowls, a carton of milk, and a big box of Fruity Flakes. They each poured a bowl and dug in.

"These fruity flakes are pretty good," Auntie Carla remarked. "I see why they're your favorite. So how did you sleep last night?"

"Like a rock," said Mikey. "I left the window open to get some air, and the sound of the ocean put me right to sleep."

"I do the same thing," said Auntie Carla. "The sound of the waves is like music to my ears. That's why your Uncle and I **had** to buy this house when we got the chance. Now I can listen to it all day."

"I hope I get a house like this when I grow up," said Mikey. "This is cool."

"Well I'm glad you like it," said Auntie Carla. "And until you get one of your own, you are always welcome to visit us in this one."

"Thanks," Mikey said with a smile.

"You're welcome," Auntie Carla said as she leaned over and gave Mikey a kiss on his forehead.

Mikey looked out at the ocean and saw two kids in the water. They were lying on boards as they skimmed over the waves. Mikey's eyes opened wide.

"Are those body boards?" he asked excitedly.

"Yes, I think they are body boards "Auntie Carla replied.

Mikey had seen them on TV, but this was the first time he had ever seen one with his own eyes.

"I've got to get one of those," he said.

"We'll go get one today," said Auntie Carla.

"Really?" asked Mikey.

"Sure," said Auntie Carla. "I have to run some errands later. You can go with me and we'll stop by the surf shop on the way back."

"Sweet! Thanks Auntie Carla!" Mikey could see that he was really going to like staying with his Auntie and Uncle for a month. He finished his cereal and asked if he could go for a swim.

"Of course you can," said Auntie Carla. Just help me get these dishes into the kitchen first.

Mikey helped clear the table and went upstairs to change. From his window he could see the two body boarders cruising across the surf. He couldn't wait to get a board of his own so he could try it for himself. Mikey threw on his bathing suit and ran down the steps and out the back door.

He ran down the beach and stopped about 20 feet from the water's edge to get a better view of the body boarders. There was one guy and one girl and they both looked to be about his age. They were pretty good too. Mikey figured they had probably been boarding since they were little. He took a seat in the sand and watched for a little while longer.

After about 10 more minutes of wave riding, the two boarders decided to head in. They came out of the water and began to walk in Mikey's direction. The boy was about the same size as Mikey, with light brown hair, which had been slightly bleached by the sun. The girl was a bit of a tomboy. She was an inch or two shorter with shoulder length blonde hair. She was the better of the two boarders. Mikey thought there was something kind of cool about that. None of the girls at his school would ever participate in a sport as cool as body boarding. They were all too "girly" for something like that.

As the kids got closer, Mikey noticed they seemed to be arguing about something.

"It's your turn," said the girl.

"It was my turn last time," said the boy. "It's your turn this time."

"Is not."

"Is too."

The two walked right past Mikey as if they never saw him. They stopped in front of a pile of towels and clothes about 10 feet away from where he was sitting. They each dropped their boards and picked up a towel.

As they dried themselves off, the girl continued the conversation

"I'm telling you, it's your turn. I'm sure of it."

"Let's just flip a coin," said the boy.

"Okay," she agreed. "You got a coin?"

"Nope. Do you?"

"No," she answered.

They both rummaged through their belongings for a minute, but neither one of them could find a coin.

"Hey shoobie!" the boy called looking in Mikey's direction.

Mikey was caught off guard. "Me?" he asked, pointing to himself.

"Yeah," the boy replied. "You got a quarter or a dime or something?"

"Nope," Mikey responded. "No pockets."

The two kids continued to look through their belongings. Just then Mikey spotted a seashell in the sand. He picked it up and held it in the air so they could see it.

"You can use this!" he yelled as he stood to his feet.

Mikey ran over to the kids so they could get a closer look.

"A seashell?" asked the girl.

"Yeah," said Mikey. Instead of heads or tails, you can call top or bottom."

"Works for me," she replied.

"Me too," said the boy.

"Okay," said Mikey "I'll flip it, and you call it in the air," he said pointing to the girl.

He tossed the seashell in the air.

"Top!" said the girl.

The shell flipped over several times before landing at their feet, top-side up.

"Woohoo," the girl shouted in victory.

"Looks like she won fair and square," Mikey said to the boy.

"Yeah, I guess so" he replied. He seemed to be a pretty good sport about it.

"So what do you have to do anyway," Mikey asked him. He had been dying to find out.

Before the boy could answer the girl interjected, "It's his turn to get buried in the sand. You dig the hole. I'll go get some water."

The girl grabbed a bucket and ran down to the water.

"Wanna help me dig the hole?" the boy asked Mikey.

"Okay," he replied.

"It's got to be about this long and about this wide," the boy said as he drew lines in the sand.

"Gotcha," Mikey said, and the two boys began to dig.

"So what's your name shoobie?"

"Mikey. Mikey Sanchez," Mikey was confused. That was the second time the boy had called him "shoobie". He didn't know if he should be insulted or not. It didn't seem like the kid was being mean or anything. In fact, he seemed quite friendly, so Mikey didn't question it.

"Nice to meet you Mikey Sanchez," the boy replied. "I'm Skip. Skip Peterson." He pointed to the girl who was on her way back with a full bucket of water. "Her name is Danielle Stone, but everyone calls her Danni."

"Okay, that should be deep enough," Danni said as she knelt between the boys. "Hop in Skip."

"Oh by the way," Skip said as he crawled into the hole, "Danni, this is Mikey Sanchez. Mikey... Danni." Danni stuck out her hand and Mikey shook it.

"Nice to meet you shoobie," she said and she began to pile sand on Skip's chest.

Mikey's curiosity got the best of him.

"Can I ask you guys a question?" he asked.

"Sure," said Danni.

"What's up?" asked Skip.

"What's a shoobie?"

"Ha ha! You're a shoobie!" Danni laughed.

Mikey was still confused.

Skip began to explain, "A shoobie is the beach version of a tourist. They're not from around here. They usually come to the beach, stay for a couple of days and go home. When you've lived at the beach all your life, like we have, you can usually spot a shoobie a mile away."

"Yeah," said Danni. My dad works for the Coast Guard. He's also a lifeguard. He said the name "shoobie" came from the old days when people used to come to the beach for the day with their lunches packed in shoeboxes."

"Ah," said Mikey. That explained a lot.

"So how long are you staying?" asked Skp.

"Five weeks," Mikey answered.

"Wow," said Danni as she packed down the sand on top of Skip. "Five whole weeks huh?"

"That should give us plenty of time to get you out of shoobie status," Skip added. "Just stick with us. We'll show you the ropes."

"I'm going to get more water," Danni said. "Pack down the sand up here Mikey, and then dump some more sand on his legs." Danni grabbed the bucket and headed back to the water again.

Skip looked very comfortable lying in the sand. He closed his eyes and laid his head back, while Mikey packed and patted the sand as he was instructed.

"So where do you live?" Mikey asked Skip.

"Do you see the red house back there?" Skip asked without opening his eyes. "That's my house. Danni lives in the next house down on the left."

Mikey looked up and spotted the two houses Skip was referring to.

"Hey, your house is only 2 houses away from where I'm staying. My Auntie Carla and Uncle Tito live in the white house with the big porch."

"Cool," Skip said with his eyes still shut. "That will make it easy for us to hang out."

"Can you show me how to ride a body board?" Mikey asked.

"No problem dude. You got a board?"

"My Aunt is going to take me to get one later," Mikey said.

"That's awesome," said Skip. "We can meet here the same time tomorrow for your first lesson."

"Thanks," said Mikey.

Danni returned with more water. She poured it on the sand Mikey had piled on top of Skip's legs and they both packed it down. Mikey began to scoop up some sand to cover Skip's feet, which still remained uncovered. Danni stopped him and gave a sneaky grin. She reached into her shorts and pulled out a long seagull's feather she had picked up on her way back from the water. Mikey began to giggle because he knew what she had in mind.

Danni looked at Skip's face to make sure he couldn't see what she had in store. Skip's eyes were still close. Danni looked at Mikey.

"*Watch this*," she whispered.

She took the feather and slowly began to drag it up and down the bottom of Skip's right foot. At first Skip's toes just wiggled a bit, but he soon realized what was going on.

"Oh no," he said, his eyes now wide open. "Not that!" Skip was trapped under the weight of the wet sand. He knew there was nothing he could do but lay there and take it.

Danni began to tickle a little faster causing Skip to giggle and wiggle his toes frantically. She looked at Mikey and pointed to Skip's other foot. Mikey took the hint and began to tickle Skip's other foot. Skip was hysterical.

"HA HA HA HA! Cut it out dude," he laughed. "I'm ticklish!"

Mikey and Danni were laughing almost as hard as Skip.

Skip was having fun, but he was much too ticklish to take any more. He began to wiggle around under the sand and eventually, he managed to wiggle himself free. He jumped up quickly shook off the sand.

Suddenly, without warning, Skip began to run toward the water. He turned around and shouted back to Mikey and Danni "Last one in the water is a shoobie!"

Mikey and Danni raced after him. The three kids played and wrestled and splashed in the waves for over an hour. Mikey didn't know it then, but he had just made two of the closest friends he would ever have, and the three of them would soon embark on an adventure that they would never forget.

## Chapter 5
# Trouble In Paradise

Mikey woke up early the next morning. He looked at the clock on the nightstand. It said 7:38. It was still too early for his body board lesson. Skip and Danni were probably still sleeping. But Mikey was too excited to go back to sleep. He decided to go downstairs for a bowl of cereal.

He walked into the kitchen where his Uncle Tito was having a cup of coffee before leaving for work.

"Hey champ," said Uncle Tito. "You're up early."

"I'm meeting my new friends for a body board lesson," said Mikey as he pulled a box of Fruity Flakes and a bowl from the cabinet.

"That's right," Uncle Tito said. "Your Auntie Carla told me that she took you to buy a body board yesterday."

"Yeah," replied Mikey. "It's a nice one too." Mikey got the milk from the refrigerator and took a seat next to his uncle. He poured a bowl of cereal and began to eat.

"Well," said Uncle Tito. "after you learn how to body board, do you think you can give me a lesson?"

"I don't see why not," said Mikey. "How about Saturday morning?"

"You got it," said Uncle Tito. "I'll put it on my calendar."

"Okay," Mikey agreed.

Uncle Tito finished his coffee, put his mug in the dishwasher and grabbed his briefcase.

"Mikey, you be careful out there in the water.

Always remember to respect the power of the ocean."

"I will Uncle Tito." Mikey replied. He could see that his uncle was very serious.

"And remember one more thing," Uncle Tito said as he walked to the front door. "Have fun."

"Oh, I will," said Mikey. "You can count on that."

Uncle Tito called upstairs to Auntie Carla, "Honey, I'm leaving for work."

Auntie Carla came down to kiss him goodbye. "Have a good day. I'll see you later."

"See you later champ," Uncle Tito called to Mikey.

"See you later Uncle Tito," he replied as his uncle walked out of the front door.

Auntie Carla entered the kitchen. "Good morning Mikey," she said as she took a seat next to Mikey.

"Good morning," replied Mikey.

"Got any plans for today?" she asked.

"Yep!" said Mikey. "A body board lesson."

"Oh yes, that's right. Your new friends are supposed to show you how to ride. What time are you guys getting together to do that?"

"I think we're going to do it right now!" Mikey said looking out of the window.

He could see Danni and Skip coming from Skip's house. They were walking down the beach with their body boards in hand.

"Can I take my board down to the water?" asked Mikey.

"Yes," said Auntie Carla. "Just be careful. I'll be keeping an eye on you."

Mikey went to the garage and got his new body board. He ran down the beach expecting to find Skip and Danni in the water. Instead, his two new friends were sitting on the beach. Skip had his head in his hands.

"What's up guys?" Mikey asked. He could tell by the look on Danni's face that there was something wrong.

"Someone broke into Skip's house last night," she said.

"Oh no," said Mikey. He was astonished that something like that would ever happen in a nice little beach town like Cape Vernon. "What did they take?" he asked.

"Some money and some of my mom's jewelry," replied Skip.

"Did anyone get hurt?" asked Mikey.

"No," said Skip. "But everyone is pretty shaken up back at my house."

"The whole neighborhood is shaken up," added Danni. "This is the second robbery this summer."

"When was the first?" asked Mikey.

"About a week ago," said Skip. "The police think they might be related."

"Now everyone is afraid their house might be next," said Danni.

"That's kinda scary," Mikey said thinking of his Auntie and Uncle.

"Yeah it is," replied Danni.

"Well I guess this is a bad time for a body board lesson, huh?" Mikey asked Skip.

"Nah," Skip replied. "I'll give you a lesson. It might help me forget about stuff for a while."

"Are you sure?" Mikey asked.

"Yeah," Skip said as he stood to his feet. A smile managed to crawl across his face. "Come on. Last one in the water is a shoobie."

With that, the three kids ran down to the water and jumped in. Skip and Danni showed Mikey the basics of body boarding, and everything was back to normal... at least for a little while.

Around 12:00 Auntie Carla came out on the porch and called to Mikey. "Lunchtime Mikey! Come and get it!"

Mikey turned to his friends.

"Would you guys like to come up to the house for lunch?"

"Yeah," said Skip.

"Sure," replied Danni.

"Come on," Mikey said. "I'll introduce you to my Auntie Carla."

The three kids walked back to the house.

"Well," said Auntie Carla. "We've got guests."

"Yeah," Mikey said. "I hope you don't mind. This is my friend Danni and my friend Skip."

"I don't mind at all," Auntie Carla replied. "It's a pleasure to meet you Danni and Skip. I'm Mikey's Auntie Carla Benitez."

"Hi Mrs. Benitez," Danni responded.

"Nice to meet you Mrs. B," said Skip.

"Have a seat on the porch," Auntie Carla said, "I'll bring you guys some lunch. I hope you all like peanut butter and jelly."

Danni smiled. "I love peanut butter and jelly." She said.

"P.B. & J. is my favorite," replied Skip.

"Good," said Auntie Carla. "I'll be right back with the sandwiches."

Auntie Carla went into the house and quickly emerged with three sandwiches and three glasses of juice.

"Here you go," she said as she set the food in front of the kids. "So tell me, how did Mikey do with his first body board lesson?"

"Not bad," said Danni.

"We'll make him a pro by the end of the month Mrs. B," Skip added.

Danni and Skip bit into their sandwiches, but Mikey couldn't eat just yet.

"Auntie Carla, did you know that there was a robbery in your neighborhood about a week ago?"

"Yes," she replied. "I heard the Robinson's had a break in. Some of Mrs. Robinson's jewelry was stolen."

"Well Skip's house was broken into last night. Some of his mother's jewelry was stolen too. The police think the two robberies are related"

"Oh my," she replied looking at Skip. "Is everyone okay?"

"Well," said Skip, "no one got hurt or anything, but like I was telling Mikey, everyone is pretty shaken up."

"I imagine so," said Auntie Carla.

The four of them sat in silence for a minute. Mikey noticed the worried expression on Auntie Carla's face. He never meant to upset her, but he felt she needed to know.

"Hey Mikey," Danni said, breaking the silence, "I forgot to tell you. Tomorrow is my birthday. I'm having some people over for ice cream and cake around 7:00. You should come."

Mikey looked at his aunt. "Can I go Aunt Carla?"

"Huh? Oh… yes. Sure you can go," Auntie Carla responded. Her mind was obviously still on the robberies. "What time did you say?"

"7:00," Danni repeated.

"Okay. I just need to talk it over with Mikey's mom and Uncle Tito, but I'm sure it will be okay."

"Great," Danni replied. The three friends smiled at each other.

"You guys finish your sandwiches," said Auntie Carla. "I'm going inside. Mikey, when you any your guests have finished, please clear the table and put the dishes in the dishwasher. I'll wash them later."

Auntie Carla got up from the table and went inside. Mikey, Skip and Danni finished their lunch and Mikey cleared the table as Auntie Carla asked.

While Mikey was in the kitchen he overheard Auntie Carla in the family room talking on the phone. She was talking to Uncle Tito about the latest robbery. She seemed very concerned.

Mikey almost felt bad about telling her, but he knew he had done the right thing.

He rejoined his friends on the porch and they all went back down to the water to resume Mikey's body board lesson. Although they were all having fun, the robberies were still in the back of everyone's mind.

# Chapter 6
# The Gift

The next morning Mikey sprang out of bed and looked out of the window. He hoped to see Skip and Danni already on the beach. Instead, what he saw made his heart sink. Rain. It was pouring outside. No body board lesson today.

Mikey went downstairs for his daily bowl of cereal. Auntie Carla was already in the kitchen.

"Good morning Mikey," she said.

"Good morning," Mikey replied.

"Why the long face?" Auntie Carla asked.

"It's raining," said Mikey.

"You're not going to let a little rain get you down are you?" Auntie Carla asked. "I'll tell you what… If you help me out around the house a little this morning, I'll show you how to have a good time on a rainy day."

"Okay," said Mikey.

He finished his breakfast and assisted Auntie Carla with some of the housework. When they were through, Auntie Carla went upstairs and returned with a 1001 piece jigsaw puzzle and a deck of cards. She made a big bowl of popcorn and the two of them sat on the porch worked on the puzzle and played cards for hours.

By the time the last piece of the puzzle was put in place, it was time for lunch. Auntie Carla made sandwiches and the two of them crawled into the hammock together; Mikey at one end and Auntie Carla at the other. They ate, talked and watched the rain fall.

Later that afternoon, Auntie Carla took Mikey to a movie. When the movie was over, they came outside to discover the rain had stopped and the sun was peeking through the clouds.

Next they stopped by the surf shop to pick up a present to bring to Danni's birthday party. Mikey picked out a friendship bracelet he was sure she would like. Finally the two headed for home.

They wrapped the gift while they waited for Uncle Tito to come home form work. As soon as he arrived, Auntie Carla made dinner and they all sat down to eat. As they ate, Mikey told Uncle Tito all about his day.

"Well it sounds like the two of you had a great time," said Uncle Tito.

"We did," said Mikey. "I never knew a rainy day could be so fun."

"It is when you hang out with me," said Auntie Carla with a smile.

After dinner, Mikey, Auntie Carla, and Uncle Tito all went for a walk. They walked down the beach past the last house and over the dunes. They stopped at the base of a small cliff where Uncle Tito found some flat rocks and showed Mikey how to make them skip across the water. He was pretty good at it. He made one rock skip 9 times. Mikey got up to 6 skips, which wasn't bad for his first time.

After a few minutes of rock skipping, Auntie Carla announced, "Okay guys, we should start back to the house. We don't want Mikey to be late for the party."

Mikey was excited. He couldn't wait to see Danni's face when she opened his gift. As he turned to leave he noticed something in the face of the cliff. It was a hole. A cave to be exact. Mikey wondered how deep the cave was and what it looked like inside. He imagined exploring the cave and finding a pirate's treasure which had been lost for hundreds of years.

"Hey champ. You coming?" asked Uncle Tito, disturbing Mikey's daydream. "You don't want to miss the party do you?"

"No way," replied Mikey. I wouldn't want to do that."

They all walked back to the house. Once they arrived, Mikey ran up to his room and changed his clothes as fast as he could.

He ran back down the stairs and announced, "Okay, I'm ready!"

"Don't forget this," Auntie Carla said holding Danni's gift in the air.

"Oh yeah," said Mikey. "Thanks."

With that, Uncle Tito and Mikey walked out of the door and down the street to Danni's house. They rang the doorbell and Danni's father answered.

"Hey Tito," he said as he opened the door. Mikey was surprised. He didn't know they knew each other.

"Hey Dave," replied Uncle Tito. "How's it going?"

"Oh, I can't complain." Danni's father turned his attention to Mikey. "And you must be Mikey. I've heard a lot about you."

"Hi Mr. Stone," Mikey said. "Nice to meet you. Danni says you work for the Coast Guard, and you're a lifeguard. They sound like pretty cool jobs."

"The coolest," Mr. Stone replied. "Come on in. Danielle is the living room with the rest of her guests."

Mikey came in and made his way to the living room while Uncle Tito and Mr. Stone went into the kitchen. He entered the room, and spotted Danni and Skip sitting with a group of kids he didn't know. To his left was a big chair covered with presents. Mikey placed his present on the pile. Next to the chair he noticed two pictures sitting on an end table. The first picture was of Danni and her dad. It looked like a fairly recent picture. The second was of a woman with long blonde hair. She was very pretty. Mikey figured she must have been Danni's mother. The resemblance was remarkable. This picture was considerably older. Mikey wondered if he would get a chance to meet her before the party was over.

Just then, a familiar voice rang out over the other kids voices.

"Hey Mikey!" It was Danni. "Glad you could make it. Come on over. I'll introduce you to everyone."

While Danni was making the introductions, Uncle Tito and Mr. Stone came out of the kitchen with a tub of ice cream and a big cake with eleven candles and "Happy Birthday Danielle" written in icing. Mr. Stone led everyone in a chorus of "Happy Birthday to You", and Danni blew out the candles. Then Mr. Stone cut the cake and put each piece on a plate. Uncle Tito helped by putting a scoop of ice cream on each plate and passing them out to the kids. Mikey took a plate from his uncle and found a seat on the floor next to Skip and Danni.

"This is good cake," said Skip as he shoved a huge bite into his mouth.

"Take it easy dude," Danni replied. "There's plenty more where that came from."

Mikey, Danni and the other kids laughed, as Skip continued to shovel in the cake.

Mikey's attention was drawn to the picture of the pretty woman on the table once again.

"Is that your mother?" he asked.

"Mmm hmm," Danni replied her mouth full of cake.

"She's pretty," said Mikey.

"Yes she was," replied Danni.

"Was?" asked Mikey.

"Yeah," Danni said. "She died when I was just a baby."

"Oh, I'm sorry," said Mikey. He felt bad for bringing up the subject.

"Don't be," Danni replied. "You couldn't have

known. Besides, you're right. She was pretty. My dad says I have her eyes."

"Yeah you do," Mikey agreed as he looked closely at the picture.

"Thanks," Danni said with a smile. "I just wish I had the chance to get to know her."

"I know what you mean," said Mikey. "I never got the chance to get to know my father."

"Did he die too?" asked Danni.

"No," Mikey replied. "He just kinda left. My Ma says 'he just wasn't ready to be a dad', whatever that means. For some reason, I have the feeling he would have been a great dad."

"Yeah," said Danni. "I think my mom would have been a great mom too. I guess we'll never really know for sure, but it's nice to think so anyway."

Danni's father stood up and announced, "Okay Danni. Time to open some presents!"

Danni's eyes lit up and she sprang to her feet. She made her way over to the chair of presents and began to unwrap them one by one. Mikey felt a little nervous when she got to his present. She had gotten some pretty cool gifts. He just hoped his could measure up to some of the others. Danni opened the gift and gasped. Mikey wasn't sure what that meant.

"Do you like it?" he asked with hesitation.

"Are you kidding?" she responded. "I love it." She held it up for everyone to see. "It's a friendship bracelet," she said. "What better gift to receive on your birthday than friendship."

Mikey hadn't thought about it like that before, but since she had put it that way, his gift seemed better than ever.

Danni continued to open her presents until there were none left... or so she thought.

"Okay Danielle," said Mr. Stone, "now it's time for me to give you my presents."

Danni's father left the room for a minute and returned with two boxes; One very big box and one little box.

"Which one do you want to open first?" he asked.

"The big one!" exclaimed Danni.

She tore open the wrapping paper to uncover a new tent.

"Wow! This is perfect for camping out on the beach!" she said. "Thanks dad."

"You're welcome sweetheart, but you still have one gift left," he said as he handed her the small box.

Danni opened the box and pulled out a gold locket.

"It's beautiful," she said.

"I hoped you would like it," her father said. "It belonged to your mother. I figured you were old enough for me to pass it on to you now."

Danni opened the locket. Inside was a picture of her mother. Danni was speechless. She closed the locket and held it close to her heart. She looked at her father as her eyes welled up with tears. Unable to find the words to express her gratitude, Danni simply gave him the biggest hug she could possibly give.

*"You're welcome"* he whispered in her ear.

# Chapter 7
# The Fabulous 4<sup>th</sup>

For the next few days, the three kids routinely met on the beach every morning for a body board session. But on July 4th, they had a forth person join their group. It was Uncle Tito. He hadn't forgotten about the lesson Mikey had promised him. Skip and Danni were happy to help with the lesson. The four of them spent all morning riding the waves. Uncle Tito didn't do as well as Mikey did on his first try, but the kids all had to admit that he wasn't bad, for a grown-up. After body boarding, it was Mikey's turn to get buried in the sand. With Uncle Tito's help, they were done in no time. Once Mikey was buried from head to toe, Uncle Tito, Skip, and Danni all laid on their backs with their heads next to Mikey's.

"Hey guys," Uncle Tito said to Danni and Skip, "I'm taking Mikey to the boardwalk this afternoon. Would you like to come along?"

"Yeah!" said Skip.

"Sure!" replied Danni.

"Okay. You two go home and ask your parents to make sure it's okay. If they say it's yes, then we'll meet at my house around 3:00."

"Okay," said Danni. "Thanks Mr. Benitez."

"Yeah, Thanks Mr. B.," said Skip.

The two kids sprang to their feet, gathered their belongings and ran back to their houses. Uncle Tito helped Mikey crawl out from under the sand and walked him back to the house.

"Thanks for inviting my friends Uncle Tito," Mikey said.

"Your welcome Champ," he replied.

Mikey felt a warm feeling inside as he walked to the house with Uncle Tito. He realized what a lucky guy he was to have such a great family.

Suddenly he shouted, "Hey Uncle Tito! Last one to the house is a shoobie!"

"A what?" Uncle Tito asked as Mikey raced off toward the house. Uncle Tito had no desire to be a shoobie, even though he had no idea what a shoobie was. He chased Mikey up the beach, onto the porch and all the way into the house.

At 3:00 sharp, the doorbell rang. Uncle Tito answered it.

"Mikey! Danni and Skip are here!" he called up the stairs. Seconds later, Mikey came racing down the stairs, almost running right into Auntie Carla.

"Slow down," she said, "the boardwalk isn't going anywhere."

"You guys ready to go?" Uncle Tito asked.

"Yeah!" they all answered in unison.

"Alright then, let's go," he replied.

With that they all turned and walked out of the door.

"Have fun!" Auntie Carla shouted as she stood in

the doorway and watched them pile into the car.

Auntie Carla and Uncle Tito only lived 8 blocks from the boardwalk, so it didn't take long to get there, but it did take a while to find a parking spot. After all, it was the 4th of July. Hundreds of people had flocked to the beach for the weekend. When they finally reached the boardwalk there were people for as far as the eye could see, but Mikey didn't care. He was in his own world, and the only other people in his world were Skip, Danni, and Uncle Tito. The four of them spent the next couple of hours playing miniature golf and arcade games, riding roller coasters and bumper cars, and eating junk food. In other words, they were having the time of their lives.

As they walked, they passed Pete's Pier Water Park. Danni loved Pete's Pier. She told Mikey all about the different water rides they had inside.

"Maybe my dad can bring us back to the water park one day," she said. "Then you can see all the cool stuff for yourself."

"Can I?" Mikey asked his Uncle Tito.

"I don't see why not," he replied. Just then Uncle Tito noticed something was wrong. He began to look around nervously. "Hey! Where's Skip?"

Mikey looked behind him where Skip had been walking. "He was right here a minute ago,"

Danni looked off to their right. "There he is," she

shouted as she pointed him out in the crowd. Hey Skip, wait up!"

"Where ya going?" Mikey called out.

Skip never turned around. He continued walking almost as if he was in a trance. Danni, Mikey, and Uncle Tito ran after him. Danni was the first one to reach him.

"What's going on dude?" she asked.

"Cooool" replied Skip as he pointed straight ahead. There was a large group of people standing in front of him. They all seemed to be watching something. Skip managed to make his way through the crowd. Finally, he came to the front of a small stage where a young magician was performing. Mikey, Danni, and Uncle Tito struggled to keep up with him as they made their way behind him.

"A magician," said Danni, "I should have known."

"Known what?" asked Mikey.

Danni explained, "Skip has always been a freak about magicians. Ever since I've known him, he's had some kind of fascination with magic tricks and stuff like that. Weird huh?"

Mikey laughed.

Uncle Tito was just relieved that they didn't loose the boy in the crowd. "Well," he said, "since we're here, we might as well enjoy the show.

They all sat down at the front of the stage and watched the magician as he performed card tricks, made things disappear and reappear, and even levitated a volunteer in mid air. The guy was pretty good. Skip's favorite part of the show came when the magician used a magic box to saw a girl in half. That was always his favorite trick.

After the show, Uncle Tito told the kids it was time to go. He wanted to get them home in time for dinner. Reluctantly, they all walked back to the car.

"Maybe we'll come back another day when it's not so crowded," he said as they got into the car. The kids liked the sound of that.

Uncle Tito started the car and pulled off.

"Thanks for bringing us to the boardwalk Mr. Benitez," said Danni.

"Yeah, thanks," said Mikey and Skip.

"No problem guys," Uncle Tito replied. "So are you ready for the fireworks tonight?"

"Yeah," said Danni.

"You'd better believe it!" said Skip.

"There's gonna be fireworks?" Mikey asked excitedly.

"Yeah. Didn't I tell you?" Uncle Tito replied. "It just wouldn't be the Forth of July without fireworks."

"Were do you go to see them?" asked Mikey.

"Right on the beach," replied Skip.

Danni explained further. "The fireworks are actually launched from the boardwalk," but we can see them from our beach."

"That's awesome," said Mikey.

"Hey, I've got an idea," Danni said. "We can set up my new tent behind my house. Then we can camp out and watch the fireworks from there."

"That's a great idea!" Skip said.

"Yeah," Mikey agreed. "Hey wait a minute. My sleeping bag is at home in New Jersey."

"No problem dude," Danni said calmly. "You can borrow my dad's sleeping bag. I'm sure he won't mind."

"Sweet!" said Mikey. "Is it okay Uncle Tito?"

"Well," he said, "we'll have to call your mom when we get home and make sure it's okay with her first. Skip, you'd better ask your parents too. And Danni, you'd better check with your dad to make sure he doesn't mind having the three of you camp out behind his house."

"He and I camp out on the beach ourselves sometimes," said Danni. "I'm pretty sure he'll be okay with it."

Minutes later Uncle Tito pulled into the driveway, Skip and Danni scrambled to get out of the car and ran home to ask their parents' permission. Mikey dashed in the house and asked Auntie Carla if he could use the phone to call his mom.

"Of course you can sweetie," she said as she handed him the phone.

Mikey scurried up the stairs to his room, jumped

on the bed and called his mother.

"Hello," she answered.

"Hi Ma," Mikey replied.

"Mikey!" she exclaimed. "How are you sweetheart?"

"I'm fine Ma."

"How was your first week with Uncle Tito and Auntie Carla?"

"Everything's great," Mikey said. "They're the coolest. Uncle Tito took me to the boardwalk today. It was awesome. We did everything. He even invited my two friends to go with us."

"Oh, so you have two new friends huh?" Mikey's mom asked.

"Yeah, Danni and Skip. I wish you could meet them. You'd like them."

"I'm sure I would," she said. "Speaking of friends, I saw Curtis yesterday. He says hello."

"Tell him I said hello too," said Mikey. And tell him I have a lot to tell him when I get home."

"I will," his mom replied. "Well it sounds like you are having a ball down there."

"I am Ma. This was a great idea. By the way, my friend Danni invited me over for a camp out tonight. Is it alright if I go?"

"Well," she said "if it's okay with your Auntie and Uncle, then it's okay with me."

"Cool! Thanks Ma!" Mikey shouted.

"You're welcome Pookie. Just remember to mind your manners."

"I will Ma," he said.

"Good," replied Ms. Sanchez. "I love you Mikey."

"I love you too Ma," he replied. "Bye."

Mikey hung up the phone feeling a little homesick. He could tell by his mother's voice that she missed him. He started to miss her a little too. However, his thoughts of home were quickly replaced with thoughts of camping out on the beach and watching fireworks. Mikey hopped out of the bed and went back downstairs. Auntie Carla and Uncle Tito were in the kitchen starting dinner.

"Well, big guy," said Uncle Tito, "what did your mom say?"

"She said it's okay with her if it's okay with you."

"In that case," Auntie Carla said, "it looks like you'll be camping out under the stars tonight."

"Alright!" Mikey screamed. "I'm going to call Danni right now and let her know."

"When you're finished," Auntie Carla said, "come back in the kitchen and help set the table. Dinner is almost ready."

"Okay," said Mikey as he started out of the kitchen. He walked into the family room, stretched out on the sofa, and dialed Danni's number. Danni answered the phone.

"Hey Danni, it's me, Mikey."

"Hey Mikey," she said. "Did you call your mom yet? Did she give you permission to come over tonight?"

"Yep," replied Mikey. "She said it was okay."

"Cool," said Danni. Skip said he's coming too. The fireworks start at 9:00, so we should meet here around 8:00. That should give us enough time to put up the tent before they start."

"Alright," Mikey said, "Then I'll see you around 8:00."

"Oh by the way," Danni added, "my dad said he could take us to the water park tomorrow, so make sure you ask your aunt and uncle."

"Okay," said Mikey, "I will. I'll see you in a little while then."

"Later dude," said Danni.

"Later," said Mikey and he hung up the phone.

Mikey went back into the kitchen. He and Uncle Tito set the table for dinner and Auntie Carla served dinner.

Mikey was so excited about camping out that night, he could hardly eat. Plus he was full of funnel cake and ice cream from his trip to the boardwalk earlier. Even so, he did manage to force down a little bit of food. After dinner, Mikey asked Auntie Carla and Uncle Tito if he could go to the water park with Danni and her dad. They agreed much to Mikey's delight. Mikey helped clear the table and went upstairs to change his clothes. He came back down and went into the garage to borrow a flashlight from Uncle Tito's tool box. Then at 8:00 sharp, he left for Danni's house. As he walked past Skip's house, Skip came out of the front door.

"Hey Mikey, wait up."

Mikey waited for him at the end of his walkway.

"Are you going to the water park with Danni and her dad tomorrow?" Mikey asked.

"Yep!" Skip answered.

"Cool. Me too," replied Mikey.

The two boys walked next door to Danni's house. Skip knocked on the door and Mr. Stone answered.

"Hello boys," he said. "Come on in. Danni is already outside with the tent."

Mikey and Skip walked through the house and out the back door. There was Danni unrolling the tent on the sand.

"Come on guys," she said. "You're just in time. I was about to start without you"

The three friends got right to work. Putting the tent together wasn't as easy as they thought. In fact, it was proving to be pretty tough, but they were determined. Mikey pulled on one rope, and Skip tugged on another while Danni read the instructions and barked out the orders. Unfortunately, the sun was setting quickly and the kids were running out of daylight. Danni's father looked out of the window to check up on the trio. He saw how they were struggling so he decided to go lend a hand. Thanks to Mr. Stone the tent was finished just as the sun disappeared behind the houses. Danni bought a lantern that she and her father always used when they camped out. Mr. Stone lit the lantern and placed it in the center of the tent. Mikey, Skip, and Danni placed their sleeping bags in the shape of a triangle around the lantern. Next, Danni pulled a spray can out of her bag and began to spray herself and her bag.

"What's that stuff?" asked Mikey.

"Insect repellent," Danni said.

"Insect repellent?" Mikey asked.

"Yeah… Sand fleas," she explained. "You'd better put some on."

She handed Mikey the can. Mikey sprayed himself and his sleeping bag, and then handed the can to Skip. Skip did the same and gave the can back to Danni.

They still had about 20 minutes before the fireworks were scheduled to start, so they sat on their sleeping bags and talked for a while. They talked about their favorite foods, their parents, and, of course, body boarding. Then they had the mother of all burping contests. Danni and Skip were pretty good, much to Mikey's surprise. Nevertheless, Mikey was still the burping king.

After the contest was over, Danni declared, "We should do this every weekend."

"What? Sit around and burp?" Mikey said jokingly.

Danni laughed, "No. I mean camp out."

"Yeah," said Skip. "We could be like a club."

"The Beach Club," said Mikey.

"Yeah, The Beach Club," Danni repeated.

The three kids smiled at each other. They were all obviously pleased with the idea.

Suddenly, there was a loud **BOOM** outside the tent.

"The fireworks!" exclaimed Skip.

Danni, Mikey, and Skip all climbed out of the tent. They sat in the sand and watched the fireworks display high above their heads. It was the perfect end to a perfect day, and an even better beginning to their new club… The Beach Club.

*Chapter 8*

# The Wooden Door

The next morning, Mikey was the first to wake up. He looked at Skip and Danni to see if they were awake yet, but he couldn't see their faces. Danni was lying on her side with her back to him. Skip was completely covered inside his sleeping bag. Mikey couldn't see him at all, but he knew he was still asleep because of the loud snoring. Mikey quietly unzipped his sleeping bag and crawled out of the tent. He sat in the sand and looked out at the water. The sight of the sun rising over the horizon was breathtaking. The entire ocean seemed to shimmer. It was one of the most beautiful sights Mikey had ever seen.

"Awesome isn't it?" a voice said from behind.

Mikey turned around to see Danni's head sticking out of the tent.

"I thought you were asleep," he said.

"Who can sleep with all that noise," Danni said referring to Skip's snoring. "Have you seen any porpoises?"

Mikey was intrigued. "Porpoises?" he asked.

"Yeah. In the morning they come really close to the shore to feed. If you look carefully, you can see their dorsal fins above the water."

Danni ducked back into the tent and came out with a pair of binoculars. She sat down in the sand next to Mikey and handed them to him. Mikey peered through the binoculars at the water and, sure enough, he spotted a family of porpoises splashing around.

"There they are!" he exclaimed. It was the first time he had ever seen a school of porpoises.

"Let me see," said Danni. Mikey passed her the binoculars. "Yup. That's them alright."

Just then Mikey and Danni heard a loud snort come from the tent. They looked at each other and climbed back inside. Danni crawled to one side of Skip's sleeping bag while Mikey sat on the other side. They couldn't help but wonder how an 11-year-old kid could snore so loudly. Danni partially unzipped Skip's bag and pulled back the top flap so she and Mikey could get a look at his face. They just wanted to make sure he wasn't turning blue from lack of oxygen. Much to their surprise, Danni had uncovered Skip's feet and not his head. Somehow, in the middle of the night, Skip had completely turned himself around inside his sleeping bag.

"How'd he do that?" asked Mikey.

Danni just shrugged her shoulders. She crawled down to the other end of the sleeping bag and un-zipped the flap. She pulled it back to reveal Skip's sleeping face. Skip let out another loud snore. Mikey and Danni looked at each other and laughed quietly. Danni looked around the tent and spotted a thread sticking out of her sleeping bag. She pulled the thread out the bag and brushed it across Skip's nose. Skip's nose began to twitch as Danni and Mikey continued to laugh. Danni teased Skip's nose again with the thread.

Skip reached up and slapped himself on the face, as if he was swatting a fly. Miraculously, he did not wake up. The boy slept like a rock. Danni and Mikey could hardly control their laughter. Danni continued teasing. Skip, finally, reached up and slapped himself so hard, he woke himself up. Mikey and Danni couldn't hold it any longer. They both burst into hysterics. Skip wasn't exactly sure what had happened but it was obvious that he was the victim of a funny joke.

"Aw man…" he said with a smile.

After Mikey and Danni managed to stop laughing, Skip asked, "What time is it?"

Mikey looked at his watch. "Ten minutes to seven."

"In the morning?" Skip exclaimed. "I haven't been up this early since school let out. I'm going back to sleep."

"Not me," said Mikey. "I'm wide awake."

"Me too," Danni said. "Let's do something." She shook Skip vigorously so he wouldn't fall back asleep.

"What do you want to do?" Skip asked.

"I don't know," said Danni, "What do you want to do Mikey."

Mikey thought for a second, "I don't know… Wait a minute. I do know what we can do. How would you guys like to explore a cave?"

"What?" asked Skip.

"Explore a cave." Mikey repeated.

"What cave?" asked Danni.

"You know that cliff on the other side of the dunes?"

"Yeah," Skip answered.

Mikey continued, "Well I was down there with my aunt and uncle, and I noticed a cave in the side of the cliff."

"Are you sure?" Danni asked.

"Positive," said Mikey.

"Okay," she said. "I'm in."

"Cool," replied Mikey. "What about you Skip?"

Skip was a little nervous about the idea. "I don't know guys," he said.

"Aw come on Skip," Mikey urged.

"Yeah. Come on Skip. We won't let anything happen to you," Danni said jokingly.

"Okay," Skip reluctantly agreed. "I guess I'm in."

"Sweet!" Danni said. "So when do you guys want to go?"

"We can go right now," said Mikey, "while everyone is asleep."

"Well we'd better be back in less than an hour," Danni said, "'cause if my dad comes out to check on us and we're not here, he's gonna freak."

"Okay," said Mikey. "We'll be back by 7:30. Come on. We'd better get a move on."

Mikey grabbed his flashlight, Danni got the lantern, and the trio crawled out of the tent and started walking down the beach. As they crossed over the dunes, Mikey pointed out the cave to Danni and Skip.

"Boy, I must have been down here a hundred times or more and this is the first time I've ever seen that cave," Skip remarked.

"Yeah, me too," said Danni.

Mikey turned on his flashlight as the three kids approached the mouth of the cave. The boys were slightly hesitant about entering, but Danni clearly was not. She only paused for a moment to light the lantern before ducking into the cave.

"Are you guys coming or what?" she asked as she pressed onward. "Boys..." she muttered as she rolled her eyes in disgust.

Mikey and Skip followed her into the cave. They had been walking for a minute or two when Danni noticed that the narrow cave was becoming even narrower. Eventually, they came to what seemed to be a dead end, except for a hole in the cave wall in front of them. The opening was about 5 feet off the ground and wide enough for one person to climb through. Skip was just tall enough to peek through the hole but he couldn't see much.

"Somebody give me a boost," he said.

Mikey got down on his hands and knees directly in front of the hole. Skip carefully stepped up on Mikey's back and poked his head through the hole.

"Can you see anything?" Danni asked.

"Not really. Pass me the flashlight," he replied.

Danni handed Skip the flashlight. He turned it on to discover an open space on the other side of the hole. As he panned the light around, he noticed what seemed to be a large piece of wood on the far side of the open space.

"So what do you see now?" Mikey asked. Skip was starting to get a little heavy and Mikey was ready for him to get off of his back.

"It's just a big open space," Skip answered, "But there's something in there."

"What is it?" asked Danni.

"I can't tell."

Skip finally climbed down off of Mikey's back.

Mikey stretched his back muscles. "You gotta lay off the cheese burgers, man."

"Sorry," said Skip.

"So are we going in or what?" Danni asked the boys.

"I guess so," Mikey replied.

"Okay," said Danni, "who's going first?"

The boys just looked at each other. Neither one of them seemed egar to volunteer.

Danni sighed with exasperation. "Fine," she said. "I'll go first." Once again she rolled her eyes in disgust. "Somebody give me a boost."

Skip cupped his hands and Danni stepped into them. Skip hoisted her up and through the hole. Mikey did the same for Skip. Then Danni and Skip reached back through the hole and pulled Mikey through.

Skip pointed out the big piece of wood he saw and Mikey turned the flashlight on it. The three kids walked toward it. To their surprise the piece of wood turned out to be a door. A large wooden door with a pad lock.

"What do you suppose is in there?" Danni asked.

"I don't know," said Skip, "and I'm not sure I want to know."

"Treasure," said Mikey.

Mikey's response left Danni puzzled. "Huh?"

"Pirate's treasure," Mikey said. "I'll bet some pirate hid his treasure in there years and years and years ago, and nobody's ever seen it. We'll be the first ones to lay eyes on it in hundreds of years. We'll split it up three ways and be rich!"

Danni and Skip looked at each other in disbelief.

"Man, you've got some imagination," Skip said as he shook his head.

"Maybe so," said Mikey, "but there's no telling what could really be in there. And I want to find out."

"But it's locked," said Danni.

"I guess we'll have to come back another time," said Mikey. "I'll bring my uncle's tool box. There's bound to be something in there that can bust this lock open."

"That's great," said Danni. "We can come back

tomorrow morning, before we go to the water park. But right now, we'd better get back to the tent before anyone realizes we're gone, or else none of us will be going anywhere tomorrow."

The three kids made their way back through the hole in the cave wall and back out to the beach. All the way home they talked about what might be behind the wooden door. They could hardly wait to find out – Especially Mikey.

## Chapter 9
# Behind The Door

Mikey awoke with the sunrise the next morning. He carefully crept down the stairs so he wouldn't wake his Aunt and Uncle. He went into the garage, grabbed his Uncle's toolbox and a flashlight and carried them out to the beach. He rested the box in the sand and took a seat on top of it as he waited for Skip and Danni to arrive. While he waited he watched for porpoises in the water. He didn't have to wait long. He had only been sitting for about 5 minutes when Skip came out to join him. Danni soon followed. They all greeted each other and immediately started down the beach. Skip also brought a flashlight, while Danni carried her lantern. The kids strangely, walked in silence all the way across the beach. Each one of them imagined what they would find behind the locked door. When they finally reached the cave, they all paused at the entrance, just like they had done the day before. Danni lit her lantern and entered the cave. Mikey and Skip turned on their flashlights and followed close behind. They weren't as hesitant as they were the day before, but they were still pretty nervous. In fact, the closer they got to the wooden door, the more nervous they became.

The kids reached the cave wall with the opening. Danni was the first to climb through, followed by Mikey and then Skip. Mikey turned and pointed his flashlight at the wooden door.

"Well, there it is," he said.

"Yeah," said Danni. "Let's bust it open."

The kids walked over to the door and were shocked to discover that the padlock was already open.

"Do you suppose somebody's in there?" Skip asked.

"Can't be," Danni said.

"How do you know?" Mikey asked.

"Because the padlock is still on the door", Danni explained. "You can't put a padlock on the door from the inside. Whoever opened it must have left."

"Good point," Mikey thought, but he still had an uneasy feeling about entering.

Skip's nervousness turned into fear as he watched Danni remove the padlock from the door. "What are you doing?" he asked.

"I'm going inside," she replied. "That's what we came here for, isn't it? Danni opened the door, "Are you two coming or not?"

Danni didn't wait for their answer. She held up her lantern and cautiously walked through the doorway. Mikey and Skip looked at each other. Neither one of them had a very good feeling about this. Mikey took a deep breath and walked through the doorway after her. If there really was a pirate's treasure inside, he certainly didn't want to miss out on the discovery. Skip was still fearful about entering, but he definitely didn't want to be left alone, so he mustered up his courage and followed Mikey through the doorway. The kids walked through a short narrow corridor to another open space about the size of Auntie Carla and Uncle Tito's living room. As the light from Danni's lantern lit up the cave, she noticed a bunch of objects all around her.

"What is all this stuff?" she asked.

Mikey entered the open space. His flashlight shed more light on the objects around them. What he saw left him amazed and a little confused. "It looks like…"

Before Mikey could finish his sentence, Skip stepped into the open area. His eyes instantly lit up when he saw what was in the cave.

"Magician's stuff!" He said with excitement.

He was right. There were all types of magician's props all around the cave. To his right he spotted a makeshift table made from stones. On top of the table there was a top hat, a magic wand, and a deck of cards. Hanging on the wall near the table was a cape, a trick sword, and several mirrors. On the opposite side of the cave sat a big wicker basket and a large wooden box that kind of looked like a closet with a curtain for a door. Next to the closet were two large animal cages. One contained a rabbit and the other contained two doves. To his left, Skip saw something that almost left him speechless. It was his favorite trick of all. A magic box used to saw people in half.

"Awesome," Skip said as he walked toward the box. He began to inspect the box like he was looking at a brand new sports car.

Mikey and Danni were just as awe stricken as Skip was. They walked around and examined all of the other magic props in the cave. Mikey looked at the wooden closet. It almost looked familiar. He wondered where he could have seen it before. He pulled back the curtain on the closet only to discover it was completely empty. He then checked out the animals in the cages. They were obviously well taken care of. Mikey figured whoever had unlocked the door earlier must have come to feed them.

Danni checked out the props on the table. She picked up the magic wand and waved it over the top hat.

"Abracadabra," she said as she tapped the hat with the wand. Nothing happened. She looked inside the hat, but she didn't see anything. She inspected the wand to see if it was broken. Suddenly, the wand turned into a fake bouquet of flowers. Although, it startled her at first, Danni laughed at the trick she had accidentally performed.

"This stuff is pretty cool," she said.

Skip agreed, "Yeah. Check it out."

Skip was standing on a step stool behind the magic box. He unfastened four latches on top of the box and opened the lid so he could look inside.

"Hey Danni! Come here," he called.

"What's up?" Danni asked as she came and stood beside the box.

Mikey was curious as to what Skip was up to. He came and stood next to the box as well.

"Get in," Skip said to Danni.

"What?!" Danni exclaimed.

"Get in," Skip repeated.

"I don't think so," Danni replied.

"What are you, scared? It's only a trick," Skip prodded.

"No, I'm not scared" Danni snapped. "It's just that... well... why can't Mikey get in the box?" She asked looking in his direction.

Mikey was caught off guard. He didn't want to get in the box any more than Danni did.

"Um... uh... I can't," he stammered.

"Why not?" Danni asked.

"Um... because... everybody knows the magician's assistant is always a beautiful girl."

Mikey hoped the compliment would be enough to trick Danni into getting into the box. Lucky for him, it was.

Danni smiled. "Well, I guess you're right."

"Yeah, and you're the closest thing we got to a beautiful girl," Skip laughed.

"Ha, ha, ha. Very funny Skip," Danni scowled.

Mikey couldn't help but chuckle. Danni glared at him. Mikey covered his mouth so she couldn't see his smile. Danni stepped up on the stool and lay down inside the box. Skip closed the lid and fastened the latches.

"I can barely see out of this thing," Danni said in a slightly muffled voice.

Skip and Mikey peeked around the box to see what she was talking about. With her feet sticking out of one end of the box, Danni's head was only partly visible at the other end. The boys could only see her from the bridge of her nose to the top of her head.

"You'll be fine," Skip assured her.

Skip climbed back on top of the step stool and began to address an imaginary audience.

"Ladies and gentlemen, I will now attempt to saw my assistant in half! Mikey, please hand me the razor sharp blades of doom!"

Skip pointed to two steel blades on the floor of the cave near the magic box.

"Razor sharp?" Danni asked nervously. "Do you know what you're doing?"

"Calm down," said Skip, "They're not really razor sharp. We magician just say stuff like that for dramatic effect. Relax. I told you, you'll be fine."

Mikey handed Skip the first blade. Skip slid the blade into one of two slots in the middle of the box. The blade appeared to pass right through Danni's midsection. Mikey was both concerned and amazed at the same time. Danni didn't flinch.

"The second blade please," Skip said, as he fell back into character.

Mikey picked up the second blade and handed it

to Skip. Skip slid the blade into the other slot in the middle of the box. Unfortunately, the second blade did not slide into place as easily as the first. It went about half way down and got stuck. Mikey grew less amazed and more concerned. Skip wiggled the blade back and forth, but it wouldn't budge.

"What's going on?" asked Danni.

"Nothing a little elbow grease can't fix," said Skip.

Skip whacked the blade handle with the palm of his hand and the blade fell into place with a loud BANG.

"EEEEK!!!" Danni shrieked.

The two boys froze, and looked at each other. Neither one of them could see Danni's face from where they were standing. Mikey could see her feet, but they weren't moving.

"Did you feel that?" Skip asked with obvious concern.

"No," replied Danni, "But I still didn't like it."

The boys were relieved to get even a semi-positive response from Danni. Skip unfastened a couple of latches on the side of the box and positioned himself near Danni's head.

"Okay Mikey," Skip said, "you take the bottom half and I'll take the top half. On the count of three we'll pull them apart."

Mikey stood at the end of the box where Danni's feet were. He grabbed a hold of the box and waited for Skip's cue.

"Are you ready?" Skip asked.

"Ready," said Mikey.

"One... Two... Three!"

Mikey and Skip pulled the box apart, and then ran around to the front so they could get a good look.

"I did it! I did it!" Skip yelled. "Woohoo!"

Mikey couldn't help but smile. It was incredible. Skip had actually pulled the trick off. Mikey had always thought the trick was done with mirrors or something, but here it was, right before his eyes. Danni was actually cut in half. Mikey walked over to Danni's head.

"Did he really do it?" she asked him.

"Yeah," said Mikey. "He really did!"

"Let me see," Danni said anxiously. "I want to see."

Mikey and Skip pushed Danni's bottom half next to her top half. Danni watched her own feet in amazement as she wiggled them back and forth.

"Are they really my feet?" she asked in disbelief.

Mikey removed one of her flip-flops and lightly pinched her big toe. Danni squealed and curled her toes.

"Okay guys!" she said. "Put me back! This is freaking me out!"

The boys quickly put the two halves back together and Skip removed the blades. He opened the lid and helped Danni out of the box.

"Thank you. Thank you very much," Skip said as

he bowed repeatedly to his imaginary audience.

Danni ran over to one of the mirrors and began to check her mid section for cuts and bruises. Much to her relief, she was completely unscarred.

"Okay guys," she said as she turned to face the boys, "I've had enough of this place. Can we go now? I'm ready to go to the water park."

Mikey could see Danni was slightly shaken up from her experience and more than ready to leave.

"You're right," Mikey said, "we should probably go."

"Aw man," Skip responded.

"Maybe we can come back some other time," Mikey assured him. "Besides, whoever owns this stuff might be back soon to lock up."

"Yeah," said Danni. "If he finds us here, he might get mad and call the cops."

"Or worse," Mikey added, "he might accidentally lock us in."

"I guess you guys are right," Skip replied. He hadn't thought about what might happen if they got caught. "We'd better get out of here before they come back."

The kids grabbed the lantern, the flashlights and the toolbox and made their way out. Danni put the padlock back on the door just the way she had found it, and the kids exited the cave.

As they walked across the dunes, Skip looked back at the cave and smiled.

"That was pretty cool," he said thinking out loud.

"Yeah," Mikey agreed, "It might not have been the pirate treasure I hoped for, but it was pretty cool."

Danni, on the other hand, was glad to be out of the cave and back in one piece. It would suit her just fine if they never went back to that cave again.

## Chapter 10
# The Burglar Strikes Again

Later that afternoon, Danni's father took the kids to Pete's Pier Water Park. When they arrived at the pier Skip noticed a crowd around the stage where the magician had performed the day before. He peeked over the crowd to see if the magician was performing again. He hoped to get a glance at a few tricks before they entered the water park. To his dismay, Skip saw a juggler on the stage instead of the magician. But his disappointment was short lived. After all, they were about to spend the next couple of hours in a water park. Besides, nothing could top Skip's performance in the cave earlier.

Upon entering the park, Mr. Stone rented a couple of lockers for them to keep their belongings in. Then Mr. Stone picked up a map of the park. Skip and Danni pointed out all of the best rides and water slides to Mikey. Then they proceeded to ride them all. Even Mr. Stone was having a great time body surfing in the wave pool. He was pretty good too. It was obvious where Danni got her body board skills. For two solid hours, the kids and Mr. Stone rode every single water ride and slide in the park, until finally they came to The Lazy River. The Lazy River was an inner tube ride, which circled the entire park. The kids decided to grab some inner tubes and drift around for a while. Mr. Stone chose to sit this one out.

He told the kids, "I'll go get our things from the lockers and meet you guys back here. We'll have to leave when you get back so I can have you three home by 5:00."

"Okay," the kids said with a slight tone of disappointment in their voices.

Mikey was the first one in the water. He hopped up on his inner tube, folded his hands behind his head, crossed his legs, and closed his eyes as he began to drift. Mikey liked the combination of the warm sun and cool water on his body. He smiled as he thought about how great his visit to North Carolina was going so far. He thought about the new friends he had made and how they had taught him a brand new sport. Mikey also thought about his friends at home, especially Curtis. He wondered what Jamal was doing right then and if he was having as much fun with his family as Mikey was having with his. Mikey thought about how lucky he was to have an aunt and uncle as cool as Auntie Carla and Uncle Tito. He also thought about his mom and how much he missed her. Mikey thought about a lot of things as he floated along the water. But Mikey wasn't the only one with things on his mind.

"Dude," Danni said, interrupting Mikey's daydream. "I've been thinking."

"About what?" Mikey asked.

"About the cave," she answered. Skip overheard Danni and paddled himself closer so he could hear what she had to say. "Do you think someone lives there?"

"I don't know," Mikey replied. "I guess I hadn't really thought about that."

"I don't think so," Skip chimed in. "There was no bed in there. If somebody lived there, they would at least need some place to sleep."

"Maybe, they have their bed in another part of the cave," said Danni. "Maybe they have a whole underground house in there"

"Could be," Mikey said, "but I doubt it. I think someone is just using that cave to hide all their magic stuff."

"But who?" asked Skip

"And why?" Danni added.

"I don't know," Mikey said. "Maybe we can go back tomorrow and look for some clues or something."

"Hmmm. I don't know," said Danni. "If that place really does belong to somebody, we could get in big trouble for trespassing." Danni hadn't yet gotten over being cut in half in the magic box that morning, and she really didn't want to go back to that cave any time soon.

"I guess you're right," said Mikey, "but I really would like to know who owns all that stuff."

"Me too," said Skip.

The three kids continued to drift along the water until they had completed a full lap around the park. Danni, Mikey, and Skip got out of The Lazy River and located Danni's father. Mr. Stone gave the kids their belongings, and then they left the park.

Mr. Stone pulled up in his driveway at 5:00 on the dot. Skip and Mikey thanked Danni and Mr. Stone for taking them to the waterpark, and then walked home. As Mikey walked up the steps to Auntie Carla and Uncle Tito's house he heard a loud scream.

"Noooo!"

It sounded like a young girl's voice and it came from the direction of Mr. Stone's house.

"Could that have been Danni?" he wondered.

He ran back down to Danni's house and knocked on the door. Mr. Stone answered.

"Was that Danni I heard screaming?" Mikey asked.

"I'm afraid so," said Mr. Stone.

"What happened?" asked Mikey.

"It seems we were robbed while we were at the waterpark today, Mikey. They took our stereo and some money I had in the house, but most importantly, they took Danni's locket."

"You mean the one you gave her for her birthday? The one that belonged to her mom?"

"That's the one," Mr. Stone said. He was obviously devastated. "They didn't get a lot of money, and we can always get a new stereo, but that locket can never be replaced."

Mikey felt bad for Danni and Mr. Stone.

"Would it be okay if I talk to Danni?" Mikey asked.

"Sorry Mikey," Mr. Stone replied, "Danni locked herself in her room. I don't think she's in any mood to talk right now. I'll tell her you asked about her, and I'll ask her to give you a call when she feels better. Okay?"

"Okay Mr. Stone," Mikey replied. "I hope they catch that guy soon and find Danni's locket," he added.

"Thanks Mikey. I hope they catch him too," said Mr. Stone.

"See you later Mr. Stone," Mikey said as he turned to walk down the front steps of the house.

"Hey Mikey," Mr. Stone said suddenly. Mikey stopped and turned back to face him. "I'm glad Danni has friends like you and Skip," he said. "She's a lucky girl." The compliment made Mikey smile. "I'll see you around Mikey," Mr. Stone said as he closed the door.

Mikey began to walk back to the house. He stopped at Skip's house to tell him what happened, then he went back and told Auntie Carla and Uncle Tito.

His aunt and uncle were more upset than Mikey expected them to be when he delivered the news. Uncle Tito hugged Auntie Carla and told her he was going to see if Mr. Stone was okay. As he left, Auntie Carla went into the family room. Mikey followed her and peeked into the room to see if she was okay. She sat on the sofa with her back toward Mikey. Although he couldn't see her face, it looked to him like she was crying.

"Are you okay Auntie Carla?" Mikey asked as he entered the room.

"I'll be okay sweetie," she said, "All these burglaries have me a little shaken up right now."

"Are you afraid the bugler might break into your house?" Mikey asked.

"I'm afraid he might try."

"I guess that is kind of scary," Mikey said after some thought.

"Listen Mikey," Auntie Carla said, "I don't want you to be scared. I don't think any of us are in danger of being hurt. It's just that your Uncle Tito and I have worked hard to get this house and everything that we have. And the thought of someone coming in and taking any of that away from us is a little upsetting. But I promise you, your uncle and I will do everything we can to keep you safe from harm. Do you understand that?"

"Yes," Mikey replied as he gave is aunt a hug.

Mikey left is aunt on the couch and went into the living room. He peered out of the window at Danni's house. The police had arrived and they were talking to Mr. Stone at the front door. Uncle Tito was standing next to Mr. Stone. Mikey could also see Skip and his family standing on their front steps watching Mr. Stone talk to the police as they held each other. Mr. Stone escorted the police into the house and Uncle Tito left to come home. On his way back, he stopped to give some brief words of encouragement to Skip's family.

When he came in the house he called for Auntie Carla.

"I'm in here," she replied, still sitting on the family room sofa.

Uncle Tito went in the family room to join her. He walked past the living room without even noticing Mikey at the window.

Mikey followed Uncle Tito to the family room, but he did not enter. Instead he stood outside the room and listened in on their conversation.

Uncle Tito told Auntie Carla what was stolen from the house and assured her that nothing else in the house was destroyed. He said the police were confused because there were no eyewitnesses even though the crime took place in broad daylight. He also said that Mr. Stone was pretty upset, but Danni was taking it especially hard.

Mikey knew why. He knew that locket meant the world to Danni and she must have been feeling pretty bad. He went upstairs to his room and looked out of his window at the ocean for a while. He hoped Danni would call later that day, but she didn't. Mikey realized that his perfect summer was suddenly a little less perfect.

# Chapter 11

# Guess Who's Back

For the next two days Mikey and Skip met each morning to go body boarding as usual, but Danni didn't join them. In fact she never left the house. The boys were worried about her. They found it hard to enjoy themselves when they knew their friend was miserable. On Wednesday, the boys didn't even go body boarding. Skip bought his radio out to the beach and the boys just hung out and listened to music. Little did they know that Danni was watching them from her window just as she had done all week.

Around midday the boys started to get hungry. Mikey invited Skip over for lunch. Skip accepted and the boys walked back to the house. Auntie Carla was lying in the hammock on the porch. She had been reading a front-page newspaper article about the rash of burglaries in the area. She looked up from her paper when she heard the boys' footsteps coming across the porch.

"What? No body boards today?" she asked.

"No. Not today," said Mikey.

Auntie Carla could see the boys weren't as up beat as they usually seemed to be. "I guess it's just not the same without Danni, huh guys?"

"No," they replied.

"Don't worry boys," Auntie Carla assured them. "I talked to Danni's father yesterday. He said she's feeling a little better each day. I think she'll get over this soon, but she's going to need a couple of good friends to be there for her when she finally decides to come outside."

"We'll be there for her Mrs. Benitez," said Skip.

"I know you will Skip," she replied.

"Can Skip stay for lunch?" Mikey asked.

"Of course sweetie," she said. "You boys wait here. I made you a sandwich Mikey. Skip, I'll go make one for you and bring them both out."

"Thanks Auntie Carla," Mikey said.

"Yeah, thanks Mrs. B," Skip added.

Auntie Carla smiled "You're welcome boys," she said, as she walked around to the back of the house and went inside.

Skip took her place in the hammock. Mikey hopped up on the porch railing and took a seat next to him.

"Have you talked to Danni lately?" Mikey asked Skip.

"Nope. Have you?"

"No," Mikey replied. "I hoped she would call, but I guess she just isn't feeling up to it yet."

"Maybe we should go over there and see how she's doing," Skip suggested.

"Do you think she'll want to talk to us?" Mikey asked.

"I don't know, but it couldn't hurt to try."

"I guess you're right," Mikey said. "Even if she still doesn't feel like talking, at least she'll know we're thinking about her."

"So when do you want to go over there?" Skip asked.

"We can go right after lunch," replied Mikey.

"Don't bother guys," said a voice coming up the porch steps. "But thanks anyway."

"Danni!" the boys exclaimed.

"Yeah it's me," Danni said as she made her way across the porch. "Did you miss me?"

"Body boarding ain't the same without you," Skip replied.

"Yeah I know," Danni said jokingly. "Move over."

Danni climbed in the hammock with Skip. She sat at the opposite end facing the boys.

"How are you feeling?" Mikey asked her.

"Better," said Danni, "I'm still a little ticked off though. I can't wait until they catch that guy."

Danni spotted the newspaper Auntie Carla had been reading. She took note of the front-page headline, **Beachfront Burglar Strikes Again**.

"I hope they put him in jail for life," Danni said angrily.

"They can't give him a life sentence for burglary," Skip replied.

"I know," said Danni. "But he deserves it. It would serve him right for stealing people's stuff like that."

Skip and Mikey could see Danni was still upset about loosing her locket. There was an awkward silence as the boys searched for something to say.

Thankfully, Auntie Carla came back out on the porch with two sandwiches some potato chips and two glasses of juice. She was pleasantly surprised to see Danni lounging in the hammock.

"Well," she said happily, "It looks like we'll be having one more for lunch today."

"Hi Mrs. Benitez," Danni said.

"It's good to see you Danni," Auntie Carla said. "We all missed you very much. Would you like a sandwich?"

"No thanks. I'll just eat some of Skip's chips," she said as she grabbed a handful of potato chips off of his plate.

"Hey!" Skip yelled, pretending to be upset.

"So what do you guys want to do after lunch?" Danni asked the boys.

"I think it's your turn to get buried in the sand," said Skip.

"Yeah," Mikey agreed. "Plus you've got some body boarding to catch up on."

"Sounds good to me," said Danni. It felt good to be back with her friends. "Are we still on for our Beach Club camp out on Saturday?" she asked the guys.

"You bet," said Skip.

"Is it okay Auntie Carla?" Mikey asked.

"I don't know guys," she replied. "With this burglar running around, I don't feel very comfortable with you sleeping out on the beach all night, and I'm sure all of your parents would agree with me."

The kids hadn't thought about that. Although they were very disappointed, they knew she was right. Auntie Carla saw the disappointment on their faces and came up with an idea.

"What if you change your Beach Club camp out to a Beach Club sleepover?"

The kids' faces began to light up once again.

"Instead of camping out on the beach," Auntie Carla continued, "the three of you can camp out in our family room. I'm sure your parents will go for that. How's that sound?"

"Sounds like a good idea to me," Danni said.

"Yeah," Mikey agreed.

"Sounds like a plan," said Skip.

"Good," Auntie Carla said. "After lunch you two go ask your parents if you can spend the night on Saturday. Mikey and I will call his Uncle Tito and make sure it's okay with him."

"Okay," said Danni. "Thanks Mrs. Benitez."

"Yeah, thanks Mrs. B," Skip said.

"You're welcome guys," she replied.

Mikey looked at his Auntie Carla and smiled. He liked the way she managed to make the best out of a bad situation. It reminded him of his mother. She was good at that too. He figured it must run in the family.

"I'll go inside and leave you three alone for a

while," Auntie Carla said. "Mikey come get me when you're ready to call your Uncle."

"Okay," he replied. "Auntie Carla," he called as she turned to go back in the house.

"Yes Mikey," she answered.

"Thanks."

"Your welcome Mikey," Auntie Carla replied with a smile. Then she turned and went back into the house.

## Chapter 12
# An Uninvited Guest

It was 8:00 on Saturday night, and Mikey was lying in bed talking to his mother on the phone. He was telling her about the indoor camp out he and his friends had planned, when the doorbell rang.

"They're here!" he shouted into the phone. "Gotta go Ma! Love ya!" Mikey hung up the phone and sprang off the bed.

Uncle Tito came out of the kitchen to answer the door. Mikey zipped down the stairs.

"I'll get it!" he yelled as he ran past Uncle Tito.

"Easy buddy," Uncle Tito said. "I don't think they're going anywhere."

Mikey smiled sheepishly. "Sorry Uncle Tito." Mikey turned to open the door.

"Hey Mikey," said Danni as she walked in the door. She had her sleeping bag in one hand and her lantern in the other.

"What's the lantern for?" asked Mikey.

"Ambiance", Danni replied. Mikey looked confused. "The lantern will make it feel more like a camp out than a sleepover", she explained.

Mikey smiled. He was pleased with her reasoning and he nodded in agreement.

Skip walked in behind Danni. He was carrying a flashlight, his sleeping bag, and the extra sleeping bag for Mikey. "Hey Mikey. Hi Mr. B," he said as he entered the foyer.

"Hi guys," said Uncle Tito. "You can put your stuff

in the family room."

The three friends walked back to the room. Auntie Carla met them in the hallway outside the kitchen. She was carrying a giant bowl of freshly popped popcorn.

"Go on in guys," she said. "Mr. Benitez and I moved the furniture around so you can spread your sleeping bags out on the floor."

Danni set her lantern in the middle of the floor then she Mikey and Skip laid their sleeping bags around it just as they had done in the tent. They spent the next 2 and ½ hours eating popcorn, telling stories, cracking bad jokes, and even defending themselves against a sneak pillow attack from Uncle Tito. At one point Danni said she wished they were outside so she could lie on her back and look at the stars. It was something she and her dad always did when they camped out.

"We can still do that," Mikey said.

He laid on his back at the foot of the sofa under the window. Then he propped his feet up on the sofa cushions and peered out of the window.

"Come on over," he said to his friends.

Skip and Danni assumed the exact same position on either side of Mikey. The three of them laid there and pointed at the moon and all of the constellations. They had such a good time that night, they didn't even miss the sandy beach or the sound of the rushing waves. In fact, they had so much fun, they practically laughed themselves to sleep.

Mikey was awakened around 12:30 in the morning by the sound of Skip's snoring.

"Unbelievable," he said to himself as he watched Skip's sleeping bag rise and fall with each snore.

Mikey noticed the flashlight on the floor nearby. He grabbed it, turned it on, and shinned the light on Danni. She remained sound asleep. The only thing Mikey found more incredible than Skip's snoring was the fact that Danni was able to sleep right through it.

"She could probably sleep through an earthquake," He thought to himself.

Mikey sat up with his head in his hands. He decided the only way he was going to get back to sleep would be to get Skip to stop snoring. Maybe if he could get him to roll over, the snoring would cease. Mikey crawled over next to Skip.

"Hey," he said as he pulled back the flap on Skip's sleeping bag. But just as before, Mikey found himself looking at Skip's feet instead of his face. Skip had turned himself around inside his sleeping bag again.

"This kid is amazing," Mikey said to himself. "He does more stuff in his sleep than he does when he's awake."

Mikey carefully began to roll Skip over in his sleeping bag until his toes were pointing toward the floor. Skip never woke up, but much to Mikey's relief, the snoring stopped. The silence brought a smile to his face. He started to crawl back to his own sleeping bag when he heard a different noise. It was a jiggling sound and it was coming from the kitchen.

Mikey crawled up onto the sofa and peeked over the back of the chair in effort to see who was making the sound. Uncle Tito wouldn't be planning another sneak attack this late at night. Who could it be? From his vantage point, Mikey could see the sliding glass door shaking as the latch jiggled up and down.

Suddenly Mikey was stricken with fear. His eyes widened as he realized what was going on. It was the burglar! He was breaking into the house! Mikey was so frightened he could barely move. His eyes were as big as saucers and they remained fixed on the door. He hoped the door would hold. Then, maybe the burglar would get frustrated and leave.

Unfortunately, the burglar did manage to break the lock, and much to Mikey's horror, the door began to slide open.

What Mikey saw next made his jaw drop. Once the door was open, Mikey heard the sound of footsteps on the tiled kitchen floor but he couldn't see anyone. He rubbed his eyes and tried to focus, but he still couldn't see anyone. All he saw was an empty canvas sack, seemingly floating in mid air. The sliding door closed partially, and the footsteps began to move across the kitchen. The canvas bag floated across the room in tandem with the footsteps, but he still couldn't see who had entered the house. That was when he realized, he couldn't see the burglar because the burglar was INVISIBLE!

Mikey laid down on the sofa hoping the burglar hadn't seen him. He wasn't sure what he should do. He lay very still and listened. The footsteps seemed to exit the kitchen and go into the hallway right outside the family room. It became hard to follow the path of the footsteps at that point because the carpet in the hallway muffled the sound. Mikey closed his eyes, still afraid to move. For all he knew, the burglar could have been standing right next to the sofa looking at him. He began to sweat from fear, but he remained motionless and silent. Just then, he heard the creaking of the stairs. The burglar was going upstairs. Now Mikey began to fear for the safety of his Aunt and Uncle. He crawled off of the sofa over to Danni's sleeping bag.

"*Danni,*" he whispered as he shook her awake.

"What is it?" she asked in a groggy voice as she tried to focus on Mikey's face.

"*Shhhhh,*" Mikey said sharply. "*I think the burglar is in the house.*"

"What?!?!" she asked. Suddenly, Danni was wide-awake and obviously startled by what Mikey just said. "Where is he?" Danni sat up and curled into a ball. She began to look around the room nervously. The thought of a stranger walking around the house frightened her. Especially, THIS stranger. "Mikey, if this is a joke, it's not funny!"

"*It's not a joke,*" Mikey reassured her. "*Keep your voice down. I think he's upstairs.*"

"*Skip, wake up,*" Danni said as she shook the sleeping boy.

Skip woke up and jostled around inside of his sleeping bag until he somehow managed to invert himself. He stuck his head out, yawned and asked, "What time is it?"

"*I don't know,*" said Danni, "*but Mikey thinks the burglar is in the house.*"

"What?" Skip exclaimed.

"*Shhhhh!*" Mikey replied. "*I think the burglar just broke into the house.*"

"*Did you see him?*" Skip asked.

"*No... I mean yes... I mean... sort of...*" Mikey said.

"*Huh?*" Skip was perplexed. "*Dude, what are you talking about?*

"*Yeah Mikey. You're not making any sense,*" Danni added. "*Did you see him or not?*"

"*Well... I saw something...,*" Mikey said.

"*Well what did you see?*" Danni demanded.

Mikey tried to find the words to describe what he had just seen, but he couldn't. "*The guy... he was here, but... I couldn't see him... I mean... he was... invisible.*"

"*Invisible?*" said Skip. "*You want us to believe that the burglar was invisible?*"

*"He **was** invisible!"* Mikey insisted, even though he couldn't understand it himself. But Mikey knew what he had seen and he was determined to prove it to Skip and Danni. *"Just follow me,"* he ordered, *"but be quiet."*

The three kids walked slowly and cautiously into the kitchen. Mikey listened carefully for any suspicious noises on the way. He led Skip and Danni to the sliding glass door. They all stood speechless as they looked at the lock. It was obvious that it had been broken into, but Skip was still not convinced that the intruder was invisible.

*"Are you sure this guy was invisible?"* he whispered.

*"I'm positive,"* Mikey responded. *"I know what I saw... or... didn't see. Well you know what I mean. Anyway, we gotta do something. That guy is upstairs with my aunt and uncle **right now**."*

*"What are we gonna do?"* Danni asked, feeling rather helpless.

*"We have to call the police,"* said Mikey.

*"And tell them what?"* asked Skip. *"We're being robbed by the invisible man? They'll never believe us."*

*"Well we have to do something,"* Mikey said. *"My aunt and uncle could be in danger."*

*"Yeah,"* said Danni. *"We can't let him get away with this."*

Just then Mikey heard the creaking sound of the stairs once again. *"What was that?"* he asked nervously.

The three friends froze in their tracks as they listened carefully. The stairs creaked again.

"*It's him!*" Mikey said. "*He's coming back downstairs! Quick, hide behind the counter.*"

The kids quickly and quietly ducked behind the kitchen counter and listened carefully for the burglar's footsteps. Moments later, the footsteps entered the kitchen and made their way to the sliding glass door. The kids could hear the door slide open. Skip's curiosity got the best of him. He wanted to see this "invisible man" for himself. He peeked from behind the counter just in time to see the now full canvas bag pass through the door with no one carrying it. The door slid closed, and the footsteps went across the back porch and down the steps to the beach.

"Holy Cow!" Skip said in astonishment. "He really was invisible!"

"I told you." Mikey replied.

"Mikey, what about your aunt and uncle?" Danni asked.

Mikey dashed out of the kitchen and up the stairs to his Auntie Carla and Uncle Tito's room. He opened the door and was both relieved and angered by what he saw. They were both sleeping peacefully, even though every drawer in the room had been opened and rummaged through. Mikey closed the door to their room and went across the hall to his room. He opened the door and saw his suitcase in the middle of the bed and all of the contents had been thrown all over the room. Now Mikey was really mad. He went back downstairs to his friends. Skip was pacing back and forth across the kitchen floor and Danni was sitting on a stool doing her best not to cry.

"Are they okay?" Danni asked when Mikey re-entered the room.

"Yeah," he replied. "They're still sleeping."

"Are you okay?" Skip asked.

"No," said Mikey. "We have to catch this guy."

"**We**?" asked Danni.

"Yes, **we**!"

"And how do you plan to do that?" Skip asked.

"I haven't figured that part out yet," Mikey said. "All I know is, we have to catch this guy."

## Chapter 13

# Shoes

Mikey went into the family room and got a flashlight. He came back into the kitchen, opened the sliding glass door and stepped out onto the back porch. He looked out at the beach hoping to spot the burglar or at least find a clue as to where he went. All he could see was an empty beach, lit by the glow of the moon. Skip and Danni came out onto the porch to join him.

"So now what?" Skip asked.

Mikey didn't answer.

"We have to call the police," Danni said.

Mikey remained silent. He turned on the flashlight and walked down the steps of the porch. He stood in the sand and looked up and down the beach. Then he looked down and knelt in the sand. Skip and Danni were puzzled at Mikey's behavior.

"You okay Mikey?" Skip asked.

Mikey still didn't speak. Skip and Danni looked at each other with confusion.

Then, out of the blue, Mikey said, "Shoes."

"What?" asked Danni.

"Shoes," Mikey repeated. "The burglar was wearing shoes. That's how we could hear him walking across the kitchen floor."

"Yeah. So what's your point?" Skip asked.

Mikey looked back down at the sand. "How many people wear shoes on the beach?" He pointed the flashlight at a large fresh shoe print in the sand.

"Dude, you're a genius!" Danni exclaimed. "His footprints will lead the police right to him."

"Yeah," said Skip. "I'm going to go call them right now."

"Okay," said Mikey, "But the burglar will be long gone by the time the police get here. I'm going to follow these footprints and try to get some more clues."

"I don't think that's such a good idea Mikey," Skip said.

"Yeah Mikey. For once, I have to agree with Skip," Danni added.

"I'll be careful," Mikey said. "I promise." He grabbed a nearby piece of driftwood. "I'll leave a line in the sand behind me. That will make it easy for the police to find me."

"I'm going with you!" Danni insisted.

Mikey stood up and looked at Danni. "You don't have to come with…"

Danni cut him off in mid sentence. "I'm not taking no for an answer. I'm coming with you and that's that."

"Well I'm coming too then," said Skip.

"You can't," Mikey said. "Someone has to stay and wait for the police to arrive. By the way, when you call them, don't mention anything about the burglar being invisible. They probably won't believe you and if they don't believe you, they won't come."

"What about your aunt and uncle," Skip asked.

"Wake them up and tell them what's going on after you call the police."

"They're gonna freak when they find out what we're doing," Danni said.

"I know," said Mikey. "Skip, tell them I'll be careful and not to worry."

"I have a bad feeling about this," Skip said. "You guys be careful. I'm going to call the police right now. That way, they won't be far behind you."

Skip went back into the house and Mikey and Danni followed the footprints in the sand. Mikey dragged the piece of driftwood leaving a definite trail in the sand behind them.

They followed the footprints down the beach, across the dunes, all the way to the mouth of the cave they had explored last week.

"Of course," said Danni. "The person who owned all that magic stuff is the burglar. That explains why he's invisible."

"Yeah," Mikey said. "It all makes sense."

"So now what? Do we sit and wait for him to come out" Danni asked.

"No," Mikey replied.

"No? What do you mean 'No'?"

Mikey took a deep breath and said, "I'm going inside."

"Inside the cave?" Danni asked in astonishment. "With the burglar? Are you nuts?"

"I have to," Mikey replied.

"Why?"

"If the burglar makes himself visible, I want to get a good look at him. I want to see how he does it so I can tell the police."

"What if **he** gets a good look at **you**?" Danni asked with obvious concern.

"I'll just have to make sure that doesn't happen," Mikey said frankly. He could see the nervousness on Danni's face. "Don't worry," he assured her.

"I **am** worried," Danni said. "I'm going with you."

"No," said Mikey. "Not this time. I need you to stay out here and keep an eye out for the police."

"Oh man Mikey," Danni said. "I don't know if you're the bravest kid I know or the craziest. One thing I do know is that you'd better come back in one piece."

"I will," Mikey replied. "I'll be right back," he said as he turned and walked into the cave alone.

# Chapter 14
# Trapped

Mikey moved slowly, being careful not to make any noise. The cave was cold, damp, and very dark. Mikey had to use his flashlight to illuminate the ground in front of him as he made his way through the cave. The floor of the cave was covered with rocks which proved to be difficult to navigate in flip flops and slowed him down considerably. He remembered the path to the big wooden door and followed it close-ly. Eventually, he emerged into the large open space where he found the door unlocked and partially open. He could see the glow of a flame coming from behind the door. His instincts had brought him to the right place. Mikey turned off his flashlight and crept up to the door. Carefully he stepped inside. The room was lit by a torch that hung on the wall. Mikey's heart skipped a beat when he saw a canvas bag float across the room and come to rest on the rock table. It was the same canvas bag that he saw floating through the kitchen back at the house. He could hear the sound of a man whistling, but still couldn't see the culprit.

The canvas bag suddenly inverted and its con-tents emptied out onto the table. Mikey saw money and jewelry pour out of the bag. Some of the jewelry looked familiar to Mikey, and for good reason. It was his Aunt Carla's jewelry. Mikey heard the whistling turn to laughter as the invisible burglar enjoyed the fruits of his midnight crusade. This made Mikey an-gry all over again, but he remained focused. He could hear the man get up from the table and walk over to the big wooden closet on the other side of the room. The invisible burglar drew the curtain back on the closet and apparently stepped inside. Mikey was confused for a moment, but he quickly understood what was happening when a door in the back of the closet opened and out stepped the burglar, completely **visible**.

*"Of course!"* Mikey thought to himself. *"It's not a closet at all. It's a disappearing cabinet."*

The burglar walked back over to the table. As he did so Mikey got a brief look at his face. He had seen this man before. The man sat down at the table and began to count the money. This time Mikey got a good look at him. Now he remembered where he had seen him. It was at Pete's Pier. He was the magician whom the kids had watched perform when his Uncle Tito took them to the boardwalk. That explained why the cave was full of magician's props.

After the man was finished counting the money, he put all of the jewelry back in the bag and took it over to the safe next to the disappearing cabinet. He opened the safe and placed the bag inside.

Mikey tried to readjust his position to get a better view. Unfortunately, when he moved, he accidentally kicked some loose rocks on the ground. Afraid that the burglar might have heard him, Mikey ducked behind the door.

His fears were confirmed when the burglar stopped and asked, "Who's out there?"

Mikey panicked. He immediately began to run, but once again, the rocks on the floor of the cave slowed him down. He was sure the man would quickly catch up to him if he tried to make it back to the beach. His next option was to hide. Mikey spotted a large bolder and crouched down behind it.

The burglar grabbed the torch from the wall and threw open the door. He looked around the cave, but he could not see anyone. He walked over to the opening in the cave wall, which led back out to the beach and began to climb through it. Mikey was worried. If the burglar went back out to the beach, he might see Danni. There was no telling what he might do to her if he caught her. Mikey picked up a handful of rocks and threw them in the opposite direction, deep into the cave. The burglar heard the sound of the stones and spun around quickly.

"Who's there?" he demanded. He began to walk in the direction of the sound. "Is somebody in here?" Slowly, he crept deeper and deeper into the cave, looking for the source of the noise.

Mikey watched as the flicker of the torch went farther and farther into the cave. When torch was finally out of sight, Mikey decided to make a dash for it. He started toward the opening in the wall and then stopped. He looked back at the wooden door. Mikey thought for a moment, and then decided to go retrieve his Auntie Carla's jewelry. He ran back to the door as quickly as he could and ducked inside. He turned on his flashlight and walked over to the safe. Luckily, the burglar hadn't locked it and Mikey was able to open the door and grab the canvas bag. He started to close the safe door when something else inside the safe caught his eye. He reached in and pulled out a locket... Danni's locket! He couldn't believe his eyes.

"Oh man..." was all he could say.

Suddenly, Mikey heard the sound of footsteps. He turned and looked through the partially opened door, where he saw the glow of the burglar's torch getting closer. Mikey stuffed the locket into his pocket. He took all of the jewelry out of the bag and stuffed it into his pockets as well. Then he scooped up a handful of rocks and put them in the bag. He placed the bag back inside the safe and closed the safe door. Now he need-ed somewhere to hide. He frantically looked around the room as the footsteps got closer. Unable to find a decent hiding place, he began to panic again. He con-tinued looking around the room when, suddenly, he got an idea. The disappearing cabinet! Mikey opened the curtain, stepped inside, and closed the curtain. He emerged from the back of the cabinet and looked down at himself. He couldn't see anything. He ran over to the mirror hanging on the wall. There was no reflection. He was invisible!

"Whoa!" he said as he gazed at the glass. He could hardly believe his own eyes.

He had almost forgotten about the burglar who was about to enter the room. Mikey turned off his flashlight and hid it behind some magician's props.

"Darn bats," the burglar mumbled as he closed the door behind him. Mikey stood motionless. He held his breath and watched as the burglar hung the torch on the wall and walked over to the safe. He opened the safe door, saw the canvas bag and, feeling reassured, he closed and locked the door. Mikey's trick had worked.

The burglar picked up a flashlight, which was lying on the table and extinguished the torch. He pulled a key out of his pocket and headed for the door. Mikey realized the burglar was preparing to leave.

*"Oh no!"* Mikey thought when he saw the key in the burglar's hand. *"He doesn't know I'm here. I'll be locked in!"*

Mikey didn't know what to do. He couldn't leave. The burglar blocked his path to the door. Besides, he was still invisible. How would he explain that to his Aunt and Uncle? He couldn't stay because there was no telling how long he would be trapped inside the cave. Mikey was completely torn. He didn't dare make a sound for fear of what the burglar might do if he caught him. All he could do was watch silently as the door closed in front of him. He could hear the sound of the padlock closing and the burglar walking away. He wanted desperately to call out, but he was too afraid. There was nothing he could do. He was trapped.

Now the room was pitch black and growing cold. Mikey was so scared he wanted to cry. His mind began to race as he stood in the dark fighting back the tears. How would he ever get out of this predicament?

He began helplessly feeling around the cave for his flashlight. He had all but given up when, to his surprise, he heard the sound of someone outside the door. Mikey was both happy and frightened over this new development. Who could it be on the other side of the door? He heard a key in the pad lock and seconds later the door flung open. Someone with a flashlight burst into the room. It was the burglar. Mikey looked at his face. He looked even more frightened than Mikey. He hastily closed the door and set the flashlight on the table. He then ran over to the disappearing box, snatched open the curtain and jumped inside. He closed the curtain and exited through the back. He was invisible once again. Mikey was confused. He kept very still and listened for the burglar's footsteps. They lead back to the table where the flashlight was suddenly turned off. There was an eerie silence as both Mikey and the burglar stood completely motionless in the dark damp cave. Now Mikey was really confused. Did the burglar know Mikey was in the cave with him? And why was he so frightened? These questions swirled in Mikey's head as he stood there wondering what would happen next.

Then Mikey heard a familiar voice.

"Right in there," the voice said. It was Danni. Mikey wondered whom she was talking to.

Suddenly, there was a loud slam as someone kicked open the door. Mikey jumped at first, but he was relieved to see a large policeman walk through the door with a bright flashlight. The policeman was followed by his partner who was followed by Danni, Skip, his Auntie Carla, and his Uncle Tito. Boy, was Mikey glad to see those guys, but he remembered they couldn't see him. They also couldn't see the burglar. The policemen stood in the doorway and shined their flashlights all around the room.

"Well, it's just like the kids said," the first policeman stated, "but I don't see the burglar or the other kid."

Mikey remained silent. He wasn't sure how he could explain his invisibility without causing a ruckus. Besides, he was the only one who knew the burglar was still in the room and he was the only one the burglar didn't know was in the room. Unfortunately, he didn't know how to use this to his advantage.

The first police officer spotted the torch on the wall. "May I borrow your lantern?" he asked Danni.

The officer used Danni's lantern to light the torch

and then hung it back up on the wall. The second officer entered the room and began to look around. Both officers walked around the room inspecting things and looking for clues. At one point, one of the officers walked right past Mikey, missing him by only inches. Mikey stayed quiet, looking and waiting for an opportunity. Finally, the opportunity presented itself.

Mikey looked in the corner where he had followed the burglar's footsteps. He looked down and spotted footprints in the sand on the floor. Two of the footprints were side by side. He looked down at his own footprints in the sand, which were also side by side. Mikey figured the footprints in the corner must have been where the burglar was standing. The wheels began to turn in his head. Mikey noticed the magician's cape hanging on the wall behind the burglar's footprints and he got an idea. Slowly and quietly, Mikey tip toed into the corner. Then, almost in one motion, Mikey snatched the cape off of the wall and threw it over the burglar's head. Then he jumped on the burglar's back and held on for dear life.

The burglar was caught completely off guard and began to stumble around.

"Arrrgh! What's going on? Get off me!" the burglar complained as he staggered out into the middle of the floor.

"What's going on in here?" one of the policemen asked.

"It's the burglar!" Danni yelled. "Grab him!"

The two policemen rushed toward the disoriented burglar. Mikey jumped off of his back right before the two officers wrestled him to the floor. One of the officers removed the cape from burglar's head and almost choked.

"I can feel him, but I can't see him!" he said to his partner.

"Okay…" one of the policemen began as he looked directly at Skip and Danni while trying not to loose his grip. "I'm going to ask this one more time, and I want a straight answer, and I want it now. What exactly is going on here?"

"Oh yeah," said Skip, "I forgot to mention that he was invisible."

"That's a pretty important piece of information to leave out, don't you think kid?" the officer replied.

"If he had told you he was invisible, would you have come?" Mikey asked.

"No, probably not…" the police officer began. "Hey! Who said that!" he shouted realizing there was another presence in the room.

"Me," said Mikey.

"Me who?" asked the officer.

"It's Mikey!" Danni yelled.

"Mikey, is that you?" Uncle Tito asked.

"Yes Uncle Tito, it's me," he replied.

"MIGUEL FRANCISCO SANCHEZ! You stop

being invisible right now young man!" Auntie Carla demanded.

"Boy Auntie Carla," Mikey said, "you sound more and more like my mother everyday."

"Mikey, you're scaring me," she continued. "You show your face right now!"

"Okay, okay," Mikey said. "Believe me, nothing would make me happier right now."

Mikey went behind the curtain of the disappearing box and emerged from the back completely visible again. Auntie Carla, Uncle Tito, Danni and Skip all rushed to his side and smothered him with hugs, kisses, and pats on the back.

"Now I've seen everything," said one of the officers.

"Not quite everything," the other officer replied. "It's your turn now pal," the other officer said to the burglar.

The policemen picked up the burglar and forced him through the disappearing box.

"Oh no. It's the magician," Skip said, with obvious disappointment.

"Sorry Skip," Mikey said. "But I have good news for you Auntie Carla," he said as he pulled the jewelry from his pockets and handed it to her.

"Oh thank you Mikey," Auntie Carla said. "But seeing you safe and sound is worth more than any jewelry in the world to me."

"Oh yeah," Mikey said turning to Danni. "This one is for you."

Mikey pulled the locket out of his pocket and handed it to Danni. Danni opened the locket and looked at the picture of her mother and smiled. She closed the locket and looked at Mikey with tears in her eyes.

"Thank you Mikey. You don't know what this means to me."

"Hey," said Mikey, "that's what friends are for."

## Chapter 15
# The Last Day

Two weeks later Mikey woke up on a Saturday morning. He wiggled out of his sleeping bag and unzipped the door on the tent. Since the burglar had been caught, everyone felt safe letting the kids camp out on the beach again. Mikey took a seat in the sand and looked out on the ocean. This would be the last time he would get a chance to enjoy this view for a while. Uncle Tito and Auntie Carla were taking him back to the train station in the afternoon. Tomorrow he would be waking up in his own bed back in Jersey City.

Mikey stared at the horizon and watched the porpoises playing in the surf as the sun rose over the ocean.

"I never get tired of looking at it either," said Danni as she climbed out of the tent behind him.

"Unfortunately, I won't be seeing it again for a while," Mikey said, "so I have to soak it up while I can."

"Do you think you will be coming back next year?" Danni asked hopefully.

"I sure hope so," said Mikey. "This has to be the best summer I've ever had. I've spent the last five weeks in a really nice beach house. I've done and seen things I've never done or seen before. I learned how to body board…"

"You practically single handedly captured an invisible burglar that was terrorizing the neighborhood…" Danni added sarcastically.

"Oh yeah," said Mikey, "I can't forget that." They both laughed. "But most importantly," he continued, "I made two really good friends."

"Yeah you did, didn't you?" Danni said with a smirk on her face. Mikey smiled back at her.

The two friends sat and watched the porpoise in the light of the rising sun until the peaceful sound of the waves was suddenly interrupted by a loud snort and a long snore. Mikey and Danni looked at each other and climbed back into the tent. They sat at the top of Skip's zipped sleeping bag, knowing what they would find when they unzipped the flap. Danni pulled the zipper open and flipped back the flap, once again, revealing Skip's feet where his head should be.

"Un-be-lievable," Mikey said as he shook his head.

Danni looked at Mikey with a devilish grin. Mikey instantly knew she was up to something.

All of a sudden, she began to shriek and scream. "EEEEEK! AAAAAAGGGGHHH! HELP! WE'RE BEING ATTACKED!"

Skip sat straight up inside his sleeping bag. Danni had to cover her mouth to keep from laughing out loud. She looked at Mikey and silently egged him to join in.

Both kids resumed the racket, "AAAAAGGGHHH! HELP! HELP!"

Skip struggled frantically to get himself free. He tried to get to his feet a couple of times, but he kept tripping over his sleeping bag and falling to the ground.

Danni continued screaming as Mikey yelled out, "GET OUT OF THE TENT! GET OUT OF THE TENT!"

Skip was completely disoriented. He couldn't find his way out of his sleeping bag much less the tent. Finally, he managed to free himself from the bag and scramble toward the tent door. He opened the door and literally threw himself out of the tent into the sand. Mikey and Danni were hysterical. They laughed so hard they could barely breathe. Skip laid in the sand, dazed and confused, but he soon realized he had been the brunt of another one of Danni's jokes.

"Aw man," he said as he brushed the sand off of himself.

"Oh man, am I going to miss you guys," Mikey said holding his aching sides.

"You know what that means don't you?" Danni asked. "That means that you **have** to come back next summer to see us again."

"I guess you're right," Mikey responded.

Skip stood to his feet. He walked around to the side of the tent where the body boards lay in a pile. Skip grabbed his board and stepped back out in front of the tent. "Well, do you guys know what I think?" he asked.

"No. What do you think?" Danni responded.

Skip adapted a very stern look on his face. "I think the last one in the water is a SHOOBIE!"

And with that, Skip took off down the beach. Mikey and Danni scurried to get their boards and dashed down the beach behind him. The three friends played amongst the waves just as they had done the first day they met, and almost every day since. As he frolicked in the surf, Mikey stopped for a moment and thought about the words his favorite teacher said to him on the last day of school. "Make it one to remember". Mikey had certainly done that. He would have plenty of material to write about in 6th Grade English class. But more importantly, he would take home many wonderful memories that would last his entire lifetime.

CPSIA information can be obtained
at www.ICGtesting.com
Printed in the USA
FSOW01n1523250917
39081FS

9 781432 793166